W9-CFP-838

UNTAINTED LOVE

IVY LAIKA

B. Love Publications

❧ 1 ❧

Ladi

"LADI WAKE UP. DON'T YOU HEAR YOUR ALARM GOING off?" I rolled over and forced myself to open my eyes as I reached over to turn off the alarm on my phone. My aunt stood at my bedroom door.

"Yes, I just wasn't ready to get up yet Auntie Marie," I said in a low groggy voice.

"As long as you've been waiting for this opportunity, I didn't even think you'd be able to get any sleep." My aunt had a wide grin on her face which brought one to mine. The pride shined from her eyes as she stared at me. She often proved that I was her pride and in return, she was my joy.

As I sat up, I responded "That's why Auntie. I wasn't able to fall asleep last night."

"Too late to try to sleep now Ladi. Go get ready and

meet me in the kitchen." She turned around and left out leaving my bedroom door open.

Today was the day that could possibly change our lives for the better. After getting my master's in business management from Michigan State University three weeks prior, I moved back to Little Haiti in Miami, Florida. I had finally landed an interview at Chez Saint, one of the most popular upscale restaurants and lounges in South Beach. The position as the general manager for the restaurant would give my career the jump start that it needed.

It was the ideal job with the perfect salary. Becoming general manager of Chez Saint would allow me to start repaying my aunt for all the sacrifices she had made for me. Whatever it took, I was going to take care of my aunt so that she no longer had to help take care of me.

Once I was out of bed, I walked into the bathroom that was located across from my bedroom to prepare for the day. My objective for today was to feel six feet tall even though I was only five foot three. Every morning after waking up, I spoke words of self-love and affirmation to myself. As I stared into the mirror, I began to speak words of declaration to help build up my confidence for my interview.

"The job is mine to have. I have the experience and the education; it is mine." I repeated it three times.

AFTER GETTING DRESSED, I WALKED INTO THE KITCHEN where my aunt was finishing up breakfast. "You look really nice. You might not only get the job, but you might also get yourself a man too Ladi."

I wore a black high waisted pencil shirt that accentuated my hips, a pale pink loose fitted short sleeved blouse, and nude stiletto heels. The pale pink was perfect against my milk chocolate complexion. My thick dark brown curly hair that I preferred to wear like a lion's mane sat at the top of my head in a pineapple style updo. Because I favored a natural look, I decided to simply wear lip gloss.

My aunt and I looked identical to the point many thought that I was her daughter. We had the same complexion, curly hair texture, full lips, and almond-shaped eyes. The only differences was her salt and pepper colored hair and of course, our age. She was also three inches taller than I was.

I rolled my eyes as I sat down at the table, "Thank you, Auntie, but my only concern today is getting my career started."

"You have the education you've been focusing on for so long. You're twenty-four years old Ladi, when will your concern be finding a companion?"

That caused me to completely lose my appetite. I stood up from our small round table that was in the center of our kitchen. My aunt's intentions were good, but she didn't understand that love wasn't my priority currently. Did I want love? Yes. Did I want someone to give my heart to? Of course, I did. That just wasn't my focus right now. School and my career never took from me, trying to find love did. The few men that I dated in the past took parts of me and gave me nothing in return. My time and energy were given to them and were both wasted. I was just thankful that my heart never chose to give herself to any of them. She wouldn't have been able to handle it. Love was an investment, and I had yet to find the one worth investing in.

"I have to go. My interview is in an hour, and I want to

get there early." I grabbed my keys from the table, kissed my aunt on the cheek, and walked out of the house feeling six feet tall. Finding love would have to wait but I wasn't going to tell my aunt that. The way I saw it, love happened when it was meant to happen. No longer would I avoid it, but I was not going to actively look for it either.

❀ 2 ❀

Ladi
When I arrived at Chez Saint, I began to feel anxious. The outside of the two-story building screamed elegance. The downstairs was an upscale restaurant that I hoped to manage, and the upstairs was a lounge.

I got out of my black Toyota Camry and walked up to the modern style building. It was locked, so I rang the buzzer that was next to the tall tinted double glass doors. One minute later a tall, dark chocolate man with a full beard and bald head unlocked and opened the door. He stood in front of me in a simple navy-blue button down, dark grey slacks, and matching dress shoes. He was very masculine and very attractive.

"Hi, you must be Ms. Thomas. I'm Saint Baptiste." he reached out his right hand.

I smiled as I raised my hand to shake his, "Yes I am, nice to meet you."

"Follow me."

He let me in and led me towards the back of the restaurant. As I followed him, I took my time to look at the decor.

5

Everything was silver and black with a modern elegant feel. It was spacious, but the dim lighting provided it with a warm atmosphere. When we reached what I assumed was his office door, he turned to look at me. I spoke to hide my nervousness. "I just want to say thank you for the opportunity."

"No need to thank me. This will be a short interview."

My smile quickly fell from my face. It was impossible for the position to have already been filled. As he looked down at me, I couldn't read his facial expression nor his body language. My outside demeanor was calm, but on the inside, I was having an emotional breakdown. "Excuse me, I don't quite understand."

"Listen Ms. Thomas, I've seen your resume and I have read your reference letters. They're all good. Excellent actually."

A smile began to appear on my face, but his next statement completely wiped it off. "That's the problem. Excuse my French, but all that shit is just words on paper to me. I need to be able to see that you can handle the pressure. I had to fire my last manager because he couldn't handle it. No offense but you barely come to my neck, how can you run my kitchen, my servers, my restaurant? Chez Saint isn't Mickey D's Ms. Thomas."

With my head held high, I said, "I may be small, but I can handle myself, Mr. Baptiste. I know when and how to be authoritative".

He let out a hearty chuckle, "I almost believed you."

Before I could catch myself, I responded, "Test me out. It's Friday night, and I know it's one of your busiest nights. Let me run your kitchen and your servers. If I do not meet your expectations, then you'll know that you were right but if I exceed...."

His eyes widened, "Exceed?"

"Exceed your expectations; I will start on Monday." Like I said before, I was feeling six feet tall, and Mr. Saint Baptiste couldn't have been any taller than five feet eleven.

"You have a deal." He looked down at his gold Rolex watch. "It's 9:12 AM. Be back here at five this evening. I'll give you a rundown of what is expected of you for the night. Make sure to wear all black Ms. Thomas."

"Yes, sir." I shook his hand and walked away.

Although I was confident in my ability, I couldn't help but be apprehensive. There were other restaurants in Miami but not with the reputation of Chez Saint. None with the starting salary he was offering. None that would give me the type of experience I needed. My degrees needed to translate to money so that I could take care of my aunt like she had been doing for me since I was two years old. There weren't any other options. I had to blow him away.

My aunt's car was gone when I made it back home. Today was her day off, but I assumed she decided to work overtime. She worked in housekeeping at Jackson Memorial Hospital. I hated that she had to work as much as she did. I hated that she had to work period. The only way I had the power to change that was by getting the position as general manager of the restaurant at Chez Saint. After I unlocked the door, I walked in and sat on the brown couch in the living room to mentally prepare myself for tonight.

I CHECKED THE TIME ON THE DASHBOARD OF MY CAR and saw that the clock read 4:45 PM. I had two-strand twisted my hair so that I would be able to put it in a high bun on top of my head. I removed my plum color lip stain out of my purse and applied it to my lips. My black lace long sleeve blouse, black skinny-legged dress pants, and black stilettos gave me a classy yet professional look. Wearing heels wasn't going to be an everyday thing, but tonight I was on a mission.

I got out of my car and walked toward the restaurant. It had completely transformed. Everything was still silver and black, but the lighting had subtle hints of purple. The bar had purple accents all around it. The dining area was still dimly lit and intimate — the perfect setting for the perfect date.

The hostess spoke, bringing my attention to her, "Welcome to Chez Saint, how many?"

"I'm here to see Mr. Baptiste. You can tell him that Ladi Thomas is here for him."

She removed her walkie-talkie from her back pocket and relayed my message. A few minutes later Mr. Baptiste walked up to me and shook my hand, "I didn't think you would show up."

"In that case, I live to disappoint Mr. Baptiste."

"I see. Let's go to my office, and I'll tell you what your job will consist of for the night."

He led the way as I followed him to his office. Once inside, I sat across from him at his desk. His office had the same silver and black color scheme as the restaurant. He then explained how I was to oversee the kitchen staff and servers. If I exceeded his expectations there would be more to do, but tonight my focus was on those two tasks. Mr. Baptiste informed me that the staff would be waiting for me in the kitchen. Thanking him, I stood up in order to make my way to the kitchen.

"Are you going to wear those heels all night?" he asked.

"The goal was to exceed your expectations, correct?" He nodded, "So that's exactly what I plan to do."

His mouth dropped open, and I made my way to the kitchen. The staff was there like Mr. Baptiste said they would be. "Hi everyone, I'm Ladi Thomas, I will be acting as your manager for the evening. Let's call it our trial run. I'm going to do my best to run this kitchen as smoothly as possible. We are on the same team which means I will lead you, but most importantly I will follow you. I will listen to you, and I will better you. Happy employees mean returning customers and we all know what returning customers mean. Although my job title may imply you're working for me, I like to think that we are working together. Any questions or suggestions?"

One of the servers raised her hand; her name tag read Ashley, "Yes, Ashley?"

"I just wanted to wish you good luck. I'm glad you want us to work together; it's never been like that."

Ashley looked young, no older than twenty. Her voice was sweet and soft. Looking at her, she reminded me of myself because she was petite but confident. She wore dark red long jumbo box braids that were a perfect contrast to her light hazelnut skin tone and round face.

"Thank you for allowing me this opportunity. Thank you all. Now let's get started."

Clapping my hands together gently, I left to have a discussion with the head chef, Pierre. He handed me an apron while explaining how he liked the kitchen ran. Taking his advice into consideration, I also made a few mental notes of the things that needed to be tweaked and improved.

By nine o'clock everything was running well despite being extremely busy. I had yet to see Mr. Baptiste, but the staff was happy and doing everything I needed them to do.

"Where the hell is the manager?! I'm tired of this disrespect!" a high-pitched female voice screamed from the dining area just as Ashley came speed-walking through the doors. The doors closed behind her as she stood in the kitchen shaking.

"I can't stand her! Why do they keep letting her in here?" Tears were threatening to fall from her eyes.

"What's wrong Ashley?" I asked with concern.

"Crazy ass Sasha is out there. You're going to have to go deal with that."

Crazy ass Sasha? I thought to myself. Everyone had the same look of disdain on their faces, warning me that I was not prepared for what I was about to deal with. As I made my way out to the dining area, I could hear the high-pitched screeching, but I wasn't able to see who it was directly coming from.

"Where is the manager? These little females are testing me tonight!"

She was blocked by a massive figure of a man. He stood at what looked to be six feet three, towering over who I assumed to be Sasha. He had a large but muscular frame. His long medium sized black locs were down to the middle of his back. When I walked around to face the two of them, I was mesmerized by his dark chocolate skin and dark eyes. He was trying to calm her down, but that clearly was not working. When he noticed me, our eyes locked for three seconds. Three seconds too long.

"And who are you?" Sasha asked making no effort to hide the disgust in her voice.

I took a deep breath and reminded myself that I was a professional. Calmly I answered, "My name is Ladi

Thomas, I am the manager of Chez Saint for the night. May I ask what the problem is?"

I tried my best to keep my eyes on Sasha, but I could feel him staring at me as if he was staring straight into me. Feeling vulnerable underneath his gaze, I was unable to shake off the unfamiliar feeling in the pit of my stomach.

"The problem is that you all always have these little females out here trying to get with my man," Sasha replied.

"Sasha, you need to calm down now!" His voice was deep, powerful, and controlled. However, it did nothing to calm Sasha down.

Sasha whipped her head to look at him, "Do not tell me to calm down!"

All the other customers were now staring in our direction. I knew right then that I had to take control of the situation.

"Ma'am, I want to personally apologize for any disrespect you may have felt. Maurice will be your server for the rest of the night. Both of your meals will be taken care of by me personally. I would also like to offer you the wine of your choosing, on me as well."

Sasha stood there gawking at me and then looked over at him, "See Ace, if I didn't act like this, they wouldn't have fixed the problem."

Ace

He was gorgeous, yet everything about him cried masculinity. His broad shoulders, muscular build, all wrapped perfectly underneath his fitted black button down and slacks. His full beard blended perfectly with his rich dark skin. His skin. So smooth. Perfection.

His piercing dark brown eyes outlined my body one last time before directing his attention to Sasha. He didn't say a word as he sat down. She followed his cue by sitting down as well. I apologized to all the customers in my path as I walked back towards the kitchen.

Once I made it back to the kitchen, I let out a soft laugh, "Wow!"

"Welcome to Chez Saint," Pierre said.

The entire kitchen erupted in soft laughter. I couldn't help but join them. The whole night had been hectic, but that was insane.

"All I did was ask for his drink order first," Ashley explained. The soft laughter transformed into a loud one.

After a few seconds passed, I decided to get everyone back on task. "Ok, everyone…" The laughter ended. "Let's get back to work. Maurice, you're in charge of that table. From now on, only male servers wait on Sasha when she's with a male companion. Also, I need every server apologizing to the customers as well as offering them complimentary drinks, nonalcoholic beverages only." Everyone nodded and got back to work.

The rest of the night ran efficiently without any more disruptions. It was now midnight, and I had yet to see Mr. Baptiste again. Truthfully, it was Ace that I couldn't get out of my mind. He and Sasha seemed to be the opposite of one another. He appeared to be mild tempered while she appeared to be short tempered. Sasha had a caramel complexion, long flowing jet-black hair and a slim model-like figure. She was gorgeous, to say the least, but her attitude made her ugly.

Unable to find Mr. Baptiste, I grabbed my belongings to leave and walked out with the rest of the staff. When I made it outside, I saw Ace leaning on the hood of his black Infiniti Q6o parked right next to my car. Was he waiting for me? How did he even know what my car looked like?

Trying my best to ignore the feeling in my stomach, I began walking towards my car. Ace did not look away once.

"Ladi was it?" He asked once I reached the driver's side of my car.

"Yes?"

"I want to apologize for how Sasha acted."

"You don't have to apologize for your wife's..."

He cut me off, "She's not my wife."

"I'm sorry, your girl..."

"She's my ex."

Ace moved closer forcing me to hold my breath. "I do have to apologize because as a man, I should've been able to calm her down. She disrespected herself, me..." he paused as he bit his bottom lip, "and you."

Before I could lose myself in those full brown lips, he took a step back, and I was able to breathe again. "Although I appreciate the gesture, it really isn't needed."

I went to open my door, and he grabbed my wrist. My knees slightly buckled, and I had to catch myself. His touch took energy from me that I didn't know I had to give and with each word he spoke I felt him giving it back.

"Can I take you out for lunch to give you a proper apology?"

I quickly removed my wrist from his grasp and said, "I can't." I got in my car as fast as I could before he could protest. This feeling I felt with Ace was different, but it was a feeling I wasn't sure I could explore. No matter how badly I wanted to.

Ace

She got into her car and drove off. Ladi left me there stuck with my eyes glued to her taillights. Her beauty captivated me. Her confidence pulled me in which made me speak to her. She was petite but curvy, maybe one hundred and fifty pounds. She had an extremely small gap between her two front teeth that many wouldn't notice if they didn't stare. I'm not ashamed to admit that I stared. Other than that, her white teeth were perfectly straight. Her chocolate skin was smooth but had a few blemishes. She was perfectly flawed. She wasn't the conventional beauty. She was unrefined. Ladi was beauty in its purest form.

"Why you are standing there looking goofy?" I turned around and came face to face with my older brother Saint as he walked towards me.

"Man, I was just waiting on you," I replied.

We pulled each other in for a hug before he joined me against the hood of my car. "Thank you for bringing crazy ass Sasha," he said as he pulled a blunt out of his pocket to hand to me.

"Chill, you know I don't smoke."

He shrugged, lit up the blunt, and inhaled it. I shook my head at him because he knew what my response would be before he offered. Saint and I slightly favored in appearance, but our personalities were different. I was reserved while he was outspoken. Nothing wrong with either, we were just different.

We also took two completely different paths in life, but I never judged him for his. He chose the streets and retired at thirty years old by opening Chez Saint. Three years later it's one of the most popular restaurants in South Beach and a few other locations in Florida. I, on the other hand, received my Master of Architecture degree from Florida International University three years ago and at the age of twenty-seven, I was an up and coming architect with my own architecture firm.

My brother helped me live my dream by paying my way through school. Thus it was only right that I made his dream a reality by designing his first restaurant for him. Because of that opportunity and his connections, I had designed several buildings and homes all over Florida.

"Why did you want me to bring her anyway?" I asked him.

"I told you that I wanted to hire a new manager, right?" I nodded. "Well when I saw her, I was thinking there is no way that she would be able to handle it. I told her that, and she offered to work tonight as a test run to help me make my decision."

"Ladi?" I asked

He turned his head sideways "You know her?"

I quickly shook my head. "She introduced herself whenever she came to our table."

Saint remained silent for a few seconds and then said, "You said her name like you were familiar with her. Anyway, yeah Ladi. I needed to see if she could handle herself as my manager. What better way to do that than to have her deal with crazy ass Sasha man?" He started laughing as if he had just told the world's funniest joke.

I didn't find anything humorous. Technically Sasha and I weren't together, but she didn't know how to let go. We had tried to make it work because of our history, but it was our same history that ended our relationship. It became clearer that I had to get her to move on completely since I honestly wanted to explore what I felt the moment I laid eyes on Ladi.

"Ain't shit that funny Saint."

Starting to feel myself get irritated, I dragged my hand down my face. He wiped the tears from his eyes and shook his head, "I just don't understand how you deal with that girl bro. She doesn't deserve you."

He was right, Sasha didn't deserve me. I made sacrifices for her when we were together, and she was selfish. While I worked to support us, she cheated with other men. Lack of quality time wasn't an issue because I made sure to balance my time between work and our relationship to ensure she was happy. It didn't even make a difference because Sasha always did what she felt was best for Sasha.

When she didn't get her way, she would nag. Her mouth was simply disrespectful. All in all, Sasha was a difficult person to deal with. When I started to date other women after our break up a year ago, she chased them away with her antics. The more I pushed her away, the more she pushed back. It was just easier to deal with her than to push her away until now.

"Is it the sex Ace? I just have to know why you're still dealing with that crazy broad man."

Shaking my head, I responded, "The sex was good, I'm not going to lie, but it's just easier to deal with her than to not deal with her."

He rubbed his hand over his bald head, "That doesn't make sense. But hey, it's your life. You know that girl is scandalous. Didn't she bust your windshield out six months ago?"

Sluggishly putting my head down, I refrained from answering. He took another puff of his blunt, "Look; I get that she brings drama when you ignore her little bro, but your girl is drama either way."

"She is not my girl!" I all but yelled.

He looked at me with his head cocked to the side, "Does she know that? She walks around claiming you as her man because you refuse to stop giving her attention. You need to either be with her or let that go."

Everything he was saying was accurate. However, my pride wouldn't let me admit that to him. No, Sasha and I weren't in a relationship, but I was still giving her parts of me that I shouldn't have been giving to her. Although I never initiated any conversation, when she called or texted, I answered most of the time. When she asked to give me head, I allowed her to.

The sex ended six months ago after she busted my windshield while I was on a date with Monica, someone I had met through Saint's wife. After she busted out my windshield and fought Monica, Monica stopped talking to me completely. Frankly, I couldn't blame her because dealing with Sasha was draining. Having apologized to Monica for weeks without any response, I eventually stopped reaching out to her. Deep down it bothered me that she entertained Sasha's foolishness.

Some people feed off drama and Monica proved to be one of those people. She was the one that initiated the physical altercation with Sasha but put the blame on me for putting her in that position. I accepted my blame in the situation, but neither she nor Sasha could accept theirs. She didn't have to fight Sasha because Sasha took all her frustration out on my windshield. Monica wanted to prove a point to an ex that she felt was a threat to what I had wanted to build with her. She made the decision to go about it the wrong way.

Whenever Monica did try to contact me a month after the incident, I told her I had lost all interest. At that point, I was over it. Taking what I could from Sasha was me being in a place of contentment. Our sexual interactions were limited to her only performing oral sex for me. In return, I'd give her attention whenever she wanted it. Sasha and I both settled for what we were getting from one another. She would never stop. Therefore I had to be a man and do it myself.

I folded my arms across my chest and said, "Saint you're saying all this but asked me to bring her here."

He pulled himself from my car and walked in front of me in order to face me. While putting out the blunt that was in his hand, he said, "Yeah, as a business move! I'm not encouraging you to be with her, but I'm done talking about that. Tell me, how did Ladi do? I could see from the monitors in my office Sasha calmed down, but I couldn't hear what was said."

Out of my control, a smile spread across my face at the

mention of her name, "She handled the situation well. She changed the server to a male server and paid for both of our meals personally. She offered wine on her too, but I declined it. I couldn't have Sasha thinking she won something."

Saint nodded his head as he listened and then responded, "She's the real deal. My last manager didn't even think to give Sasha a male server whenever ya'll use to come here. Maurice told me that he or another male server are the only ones allowed to serve you and her from now on."

"There isn't a her and I. There's definitely not a from now on. We aren't together. Saint, I only brought her here because you asked me to. Seriously though, you really thinking about hiring Ladi?" As if it were possible, my smile grew wider.

"What got you smiling like that?" He asked.

"Just thinking Saint."

"Nah bro, I know that face. Stay away from Ladi Ace. I'm not trying to lose her as a manager because of crazy ass Sasha." he said with a scowl painted on his face.

I wasn't listening to anything he had to say because I had to get to know Ladi. Why I felt like I needed her close. Why I couldn't stop staring at her when I first laid eyes on her. Why she had that effect on me, nothing could stop me from getting my answers.

I lied, "Chill, it's not like that. So, are you going to hire her?"

"No, it's exactly like that. She met her part of the deal, so yeah, I'm hiring her."

I pulled out my wallet, taking out two one-hundred-dollar bills. "This is for our meal tonight, add it to her first check for me. She shouldn't have had to pay for our food."

He took the money from me, "Bet but I'm about to head home. It's past midnight, and I can't keep the wifey waiting. She's been with the twins all day. We'll catch up tomorrow."

Saint had two-year-old twins, Saint Jr and Heaven. He and his wife agreed to wait until he was completely out of the game to have children. It was crazy watching him be a father to toddlers at thirty-three years old.

"Alright, bet."

We hugged, and Saint walked to his car. As I got into my car and started it, thoughts of Ladi flooded my mind. Whatever it took to get to know her, I was willing to do.

4

Ace

Buzz Buzz Buzz

The vibration of my phone brought me out of my sleep. The sun was shining through the bedroom window of my two-bedroom condo in South Beach. It wouldn't be my home for too much longer since I had finished the design for my own house. It was currently in the process of being built.

When I reached over to answer my phone, Sasha's name appeared on the screen. I pushed decline and sat it back on the nightstand. I closed my eyes and laid down with my hands behind my head. As I thought back to the conversation I had with Saint last night, it was clear that I had to cut all ties with Sasha today. Not only because I wanted to pursue Ladi but because I knew Sasha wasn't the one. Sasha's love was superficial and conditional. That wasn't the type of love I was built for.

Boom Boom Boom

The loud banging on the front door couldn't be anyone but one person. Getting out of my king size bed, I walked out of my room only wearing a pair of gray boxer briefs. Once I made it to the living room of my condo, I opened the door not even bothering to look out the peephole.

"So, this is how we're doing it Ace?" Sasha screamed. She stood at the door with a frown. Sasha was five feet eight and slim with beautiful green eyes. Her caramel colored skin was blemish free, but it was the freckles on her high cheekbones that I had loved the most. At twenty-three, her beauty mattered more to me than I cared to admit. However, at twenty-seven years old, I couldn't care less about her looks. Her looks were the only thing she had to offer. She didn't have any drive or ambition in life.

Sasha and I met on campus right before I started my master's program at FIU. She led me to believe she was a student as well. By the time I found out the truth, I had already fallen in what I had thought was love with her. She wasn't a student; she wasn't working, Sasha was simply living. She had a hold on me that dictated my every move. I took care of her because once again she led me to believe she was something she wasn't, loyal. After dating her for almost three years, I found out that Sasha cheated on me with at least three men multiple times. Apparently, that was how she afforded her lifestyle. That's when I realized it was time for us to break up.

I needed someone humble with a pure heart. Someone with a soul even purer than her heart. Someone I could have a conversation with about the current political climate of America and turn around and have another one about the newest episode of Blackish. Sasha wasn't that person. No matter how hard she tried to be, she would never be that person for me.

Leaving her standing at the door, I made my way towards my black leather sectional. Continuing to deal with Sasha wasn't an option anymore. "Why are you here Sasha?"

I heard the door close. "Since when did I need a reason to come here Ace?" She asked walking around the sectional.

And that right there was the reason I needed to cut Sasha off entirely. At first, I never meant to lead Sasha on, but clearly, the attention that I was giving her had her believing that she had authority over me and my home. We ended our relationship a year ago because of her infidelity. But because I gave her attention she didn't earn, she acted the way she did. Even though I dated a couple of women within the first six months we were broken up, Sasha ruined them for me, and I let her. They honestly weren't worth the crazy that Sasha brought.

Now I focused on my career only. Letting Sasha give me head every now and again seemed to work in the beginning. Recently, I started to regret it because she would go back to acting crazy afterward. Her acting senselessly only led to me cutting her off for a couple of days, which later became our cycle.

She was my familiarity which was why I kept going back to her. I didn't want to deal with anyone new. Giving any new energy to another woman until I found my wife was something I refused to do. There's nothing wrong with familiarity if that person was yours to have. Sasha wasn't mine, and I certainly was not hers. Sasha knew the situation but never fully accepted it. Taking away the energy I was wasting on Sasha was the first step to moving on.

"Since a year ago when I broke up with you, that's when." I finally responded to her.

She put her hands on her slim hips and huffed dramatically, "Don't be like that. We were just on a date last night."

"We weren't on a date. Saint and I were supposed to meet up. I took you along because I was hungry, and you wanted to hang out. We discussed that already." She didn't need to know my brother specifically requested for her nor the reason why.

"Whatever." She rolled her eyes "You didn't even come back over last night like I thought you were going to."

After dropping Sasha off at home, I agreed to go back to her house, but after seeing Ladi in the parking lot, my goal was getting to know her. Sasha was an unnecessary distraction. "Why do you do this? Sasha, I can't continue like this with you. We've been broken up a year now. I can't keep giving you pieces of me. We need to cut all ties and move on."

Her face turned red, and her high-pitched voice was laced with venom, "Move on for what? I've been throwing myself at you every day for months, but you are choosing not to take it. Are you seeing someone else Ace?"

Sitting up straight, I dragged my right hand down my face to calm myself down because I knew the drama that was coming. "Sasha, I'm not messing with anyone else. I'm tired of just receiving oral sex from you. I need more than that. You know that we both know that. I don't trust you, so I can't be with you. You ripped my heart out of my chest and expected that to be fixed by throwing pussy at me? The same pussy you were going around giving to other men?"

Sadness filled her eyes, but I was done. I continued, "You can't honestly be serious right now. I gave you every part of me. You chose to shit on me constantly. You disrespected me, you lied, cheated, and even tried to trap me. Every time I tried to move on, you ruined it. That's stopping today Sasha."

Two years into our relationship, I walked in on her poking holes in my condoms. My biggest regret was not ending it with her then. Instead, I accepted her apology and excuses. Continuing to love a woman that didn't know the meaning of love was the biggest mistake I had ever made. She claimed that a baby was her guarantee what she would never lose me. That was a clear red flag, but I ignored it because she explained that it was her way of preserving our love. That wasn't love though; it was control.

"Don't do this Ace, you know I love you. I just have a funny way of showing it."

All I could do was shake my head, "Your love is about having control. It's conditional, and that's not a love that lasts a lifetime, Sasha. You can't offer me anything different from that. I was wrong for taking what I could get from you, and I'm sorry about that. However, you need to let go because I did. A year ago."

"We were just sleeping together six months ago, and now you're switching up on me. I'm not going to let that happen Ace!"

Sasha said six months as if it was equivalent to yesterday. Throwing her purse on the wooden floor, she dropped to her knees. Before I could even process what she was doing she had her hands around my shaft and out of my boxer briefs. Quickly putting it inside her warm mouth, it hardened instantly. My breathing became heavy, and my body reacted to her wet mouth the way it always did. Stomach caved in — pulse racing. Head leaned back. Eyes closed. As badly as my body wanted her to continue, I had to stop her. Pulling Sasha from my lap by her hair, I watched as she wiped the saliva from her lips and chin.

"Sasha, stop. You need to let me go so that we both can really move on. I want the love that you're incapable of giving to me. What you have for me isn't love."

I stood up, fixed myself, and pulled her up to my chest, "Let me find the love that I've been craving. There's no more back and forth between us. You need to chill with that crazy shit. No more chasing females away because we've been done. I just need you to finally accept it."

Snatching herself from my grip, she picked her purse up from the floor with a look of embarrassment and walked towards the door. Maybe she finally understood what I had been feeling for a whole year. Maybe it took me seeing Ladi to finally just be done with Sasha's foolishness. Sasha brought chaos, and I was praying that the peace that I saw in Ladi's eyes would drown it out.

She opened the front door, looked back, and said, "Tell whoever she is, I'm coming for her." She walked out before slamming the door behind her.

Nothing Sasha did or said surprised me anymore. Nevertheless, I couldn't continue giving her any part of me anymore knowing that she wasn't the one and Ladi could be.

❦ 5 ❦

Ladi

"I DIDN'T THINK I WOULD SEE YOU AGAIN…SO SOON."

That voice had been stuck in my head since last night. Ace. He stared at me with his dark brown eyes that pierced my soul the very first time our eyes met. His massive body towered over mine as he looked down at me. I stood there speechless with a shopping basket in my hand and my mouth slightly opened in awe. He wore black slacks, black loafers, and a dark gray button down and his locs were up in a styled updo bun. We were at Zubi Supermarket, a grocery store that sold Caribbean foods and the best fresh meat in Little Haiti.

"Do you remember me?" Ace asked taking a step towards me.

"Ace, right?"

He smiled, and my heart began beating hard inside my

chest. The wider his smile grew, the harder my heart beat. Threatening to leave the home it had known for twenty-four years to jump into the hands of a stranger.

"Right, I'm glad you remember me. Do you normally shop at Zubi?" he asked.

"Yes, my aunt's day for grocery shopping is Saturdays. It's something she kept from Haiti. I'm grocery shopping for her today since she had to work."

His eyes lit up, "So you're Haitian?"

Laughing at his excitement, I replied, "Yes. I was born here, but my mom's family is from Haiti."

"That's dope. My parents are from St Lucia." He said as he reached for my basket and I let him.

Our conversation began to flow effortlessly. I found myself wanting to hear his voice more and more. "I've always wanted to visit there. Do you live in little Haiti or were you just shopping? I noticed you don't have anything of your own in your hands."

"I actually was about to grab lunch next door at Gayou's when I noticed your car. I decided to come in here instead to ask you to lunch."

Gayou's was a small Haitian restaurant that served a few other dishes as well. I blushed thinking about him enjoying Haitian food. My mind drifted to thoughts of preparing Haitian food for him one day.

Ace licked his lips and continued, "Are you thinking about cooking for me?"

"No, I was thinking that it's nice that you like Haitian food." I lied.

"Sure you were Di." he winked at me.

Di? He was comfortable enough with me to shorten my already short name, and I chose not to question it. The grin that he wore on his face made me blush even more. It was like he read my thoughts to see right through my lie.

"So, are you done?" He asked pointing at my basket that was now in his hand.

I nodded and reached for the basket. He pulled it back and said, "I'll go pay, and we can go grab lunch."

"I can't let you do that," I told him reaching for the basket.

Again, he pulled it back and responded, "You can, and you will."

With that, he turned around and walked towards the register leaving me standing there with my mouth now wide open. I watched as he made it to the register and started to unload my basket. My feet wouldn't move. My mouth couldn't make a sound. I was completely fascinated by Ace. His mere presence had put me in a trance that only he could remove me from. Everything about him had me stuck. His pearly white teeth. His masculine scent. His locs that he wore like a crown. His big and tall build. His dark rich skin. Everything.

As he walked back over to me after paying for my groceries, the world around me started moving again the minute he was near. Those minutes apart from him had everything around me standing still and only his presence made it make sense for them to start to move again.

"Are you ready for lunch?"

"I'm not dressed for lunch," I answered looking down at my clothes.

My natural curls that I had parted on the left side were loose and wild hanging past my shoulders. I wore a green unisex Michigan State University T-shirt with white writing, distressed denim shorts, and white flip flops. There wasn't a reason to get dressed up because I was only making a quick run to the store for my aunt.

"You're perfect." The sincerity in his eyes spoke louder than his words.

Taking a step forward he closed the space between us. He grabbed my chin and lifted my head with his left hand while he held my bags with his right. "You are perfect Ladi."

I had been called Ladi my entire life but coming from him it felt like he was the first person to say it. As if until today, no one ever said Ladi correctly. He ruined it for everyone that said it before and for those who would say it after. Ace let go of my chin, took a step back, and grabbed my right hand with his left. His large hand wrapped around my hand warmed my whole body. This was his third time touching me, and each touch had brought feelings I couldn't explain. Feelings that I had never felt before.

When we made it outside, I opened the trunk of my car for Ace to put the groceries in. "How much do I owe you?" I asked after he finished putting them in

Ace looked at me as if I had insulted him. "Please don't ever disrespect me like that Ladi. Now, we're going to walk next door to Gayou's and eat lunch. That's all I need from you..." he paused for a few seconds and continued, "for now."

"I wasn't trying to disrespect you."

Ace didn't respond. Instead, he grabbed my left hand, and we walked next door to Gayou's. Once we were inside the restaurant, we were seated in the far back corner per Ace's request. He pulled out my seat for me to sit down. After I was seated, he went around and sat across from me. The waitress came and took our order shortly after. We both ordered water to drink and stew chicken with red beans and rice for lunch. I looked up from my menu only to catch Ace staring at me once again. `

"Why do you do that? Why do you just stare at me?" I asked him.

Completely ignoring my question, he said "Look, it's important for me to be a man even if I'm not your man. When I do something for you, don't question it, don't fight it, just accept it."

I wanted to tell him that I couldn't accept anything from him not knowing what he wanted in return. I opened my mouth, but the only word that came out was, "Ok."

The waitress returned, sat our waters on the table and walked away. He took a sip of his water, smiled widely, and said, "Good. Now tell me about yourself."

Not knowing exactly what he wanted to know, I opted to keep it general. "I'm twenty-four years old. Born and raised in Little Haiti. My aunt has raised me since I was two years old after my mom passed away. My dad died before I was born, so I never knew him. I guess technically, I never knew my mom either."

Ace stood and walked over to take the seat next to me. He lifted his hand and placed it on my left knee. The small gesture took away my sorrow and brought me to a place of serenity. Serenity I didn't know I needed until he brought it to me

I continued, "I'm an only child. I graduated from FIU with my bachelor's in hospitality and then went on to obtain my Master's in business management from Michigan State University."

He looked down at my shirt with his hand still on my knee and returned his eyes back up to my face. "I moved back to Miami three weeks ago for a job interview. At Chez Saint actually."

My brows furrowed as my body tensed up recalling my first encounter with him at the restaurant. He shouldn't have been here with me if he clearly had a situation he was preoccupied with. Ace must've sensed something was wrong because he moved his hand from my knee up to the middle of my thigh.

"Why are you single?" He asked.

"Truthfully?"

"I always want the truth from you Di," he answered.

I let out a deep breath, hung my head, and began explaining, "Truthfully, I've always been single. My focus was always school and now my career. I've dated a couple of men here and there, but nothing came from them. So, I decided to stay focused on other parts of my life. I was giving them my time and energy. It was time and energy wasted. Although I'm in love with love itself, I've never known love other than the one I receive from my aunt."

He squeezed my thigh, "So you're a virgin?"

I popped my head up and answered without hesitation, "No, that's not what I said. How did you even...can we change the subject please?"

He chuckled and shook his head, "I'm twenty-seven and an architect. Coincidently, I received my Master's in Architecture three years ago from FIU. I'm originally from Tennessee, but I moved to Miami to attend FIU for my bachelor's and master's. Decided to make it my permanent home. My parents are still married and moved back to St. Lucia last year. I aspire to have a relationship like theirs one day."

Everything in me wanted to ask about his current relationship status. He claimed that Sasha was his ex, but they were on a date yesterday. I even remembered her referring to him as her man. The problem was, I didn't know if I had the right to. That still didn't stop a part of me from wanting to know. Before I could get the chance to ask, the waitress came with our food. She sat our plates on the table, and we thanked her before she walked away. Ace stood up from the seat next to me and returned to his original place across from me.

I didn't want to overstep any boundaries, so I withheld my questions concerning his ex. He didn't owe me an explanation because all we were doing was having lunch together — nothing more, nothing less. My best option was to ignore my growing feelings and take this for what it was, a friendly lunch.

"So how did you know that was my car last night?"

"I didn't. I was actually waiting on someone, and I just so happened to park next to your car," he replied.

Completely mortified for assuming he had been waiting on me, I looked down at my plate. Ace must've caught on to what I was thinking. He put his fork down, reaching for both of my hands with his, "It was fate Ladi."

He offered me a sneaky smile, and he squeezed my hands, "I'm just glad you agreed to our first date. Remember this date forever Di, May twenty-sixth."

I looked at him with squinted eyes and asked, "Our first date?"

"Yes, this is our first date." The confidence that resonated from the bass of his voice sent chills down my spine.

He released my hands as I drowned in his eyes hoping to find the truth. This was more than a friendly lunch like I originally thought. Ace made that clear to me. From when our eyes connected, I feared what I felt. Not wanting to get ahead of myself I wrote my feelings off as admiration for his good looks because jumping to conclusions was how

33

women always ended up with a broken heart and hurt feelings.

We continued making small talk while enjoying our food. Our connection was organic. Everything about it felt unreal, yet here I was sitting across from this man, letting me know that it was indeed real. I hadn't planned to open up to him as much I was, but he made it easy. Our vibe was everything it was meant to be; it was pure. We didn't feel new; we felt like the possibility of forever.

"How did you get the name Ladi?" Ace asked.

Believe it or not Ace was the first person to ask me that question. Most people just wanted to know if that was, in fact, my real name and when I confirmed that it was, they didn't think too much about it. Letting out a soft sigh, I replied, "My aunt told me that when my dad found out I was a girl he referred to me as his little lady. When I was born my mom named me Ladi with an I because it felt right looking at me. It was her way of honoring him."

"It fits you. I like it," he said.

We continued with our light conversation, and I realized Ace had to be the first person ever to take this much interest in me. He continued to ask me question after question. I found myself falling deeper into him. Every minute that we spent together I felt myself connecting with him in a way that I hadn't connected with anyone before — not my aunt nor my best friend, Chasity.

"Tell me something random about yourself Di," he said with a smile stretched as wide as he had my heart open.

"Like what?" I asked.

He shrugged and replied, "Like something random. Something that not many people know."

"Um...I collect cards." I said softly.

"Cards?"

"Yes, like birthday cards, holiday cards. I collect greeting cards."

His facial expression showed his curiousness, so I continued, "Think about it, someone spends his or her time to find something that will express exactly how he or she feels. And at times, it's not enough, so they have to add to it."

He nodded his head and listened attentively as I spoke, "A greeting card is more than the words, it's a gesture within itself. It's the time spent getting it, the words written in it, the added words, and then giving it to someone you feel is worthy of those words and time spent. Words are more important than we think because they hold a lot of power. They have control over our actions and emotions."

"That's a lot to think about a card."

Shrugging my shoulders, I said, "To many, yes. But to me, no."

Ace rubbed his beard as if he were contemplating something and nodded. "I get it. It makes a lot of sense. Tell me Di, what are your career goals?"

"Chez Saint is the first step on my ladder of success. In five years, I want to start my own chain of restaurants. Chez Saint is a great start to that. The salary is exactly what I need, and the experience I will gain is worth more than that. I don't want to take a loan from the bank because I need to take care of my aunt for once. Chez Saint will help me do that and save up to get a small location in a few years. Management is my passion, but it's only a small part of the bigger plan. I worked hard to get to where I am, but there's more to it than just being a manager. Ownership is the goal and management is the pathway to it. I refuse to let anything take that from me or get in the way of it."

My smile took over my entire face. Management and

opening my own chain of restaurants were my passions. No man had ever cared to ask about my goals the way Ace was doing. He wasn't asking just to ask, he was showing actual interest.

"You really are perfect Di. You have ambition. You know exactly what you want, and you aren't scared to put in the work either. That's truly hard to come by." He reached over the table and held my hand.

"Really Ace?" a piercing female voice yelled causing us to stop our conversation. When I turn around, who I believed to be Sasha was walking directly towards us. I tried to pull my hand away, but Ace wouldn't let go. By the time Sasha made it to our table Ace's eyes went from dark brown to black.

"Are you really out here messing with the help?" she asked while turning her nose up at me.

The help? Before I could respond, Ace responded, still failing to release of my hand. "Sasha, I've tried to be respectful, but you need to leave now."

"You weren't saying that this morning when your dick was in my mouth, were you?" she said with both hands now sitting on her slender hips.

Ace jumped up quick finally letting go of my hand, and I took it as my signal to leave. Never had I argued with a female over a man and I hadn't planned on starting today. I watched them argue for a minute not even bothering to listen to what they were saying. None of it was important to me.

Before grabbing my keys from the table, I pulled sixty dollars out of my wallet that was attached to it and laid it on the table. It was enough to cover my meal and the groceries that he had purchased earlier.

The second I stood up to leave, Ace looked at me and asked, "Where are you going Di?"

I ignored him, turned towards the door, and started to walk away. I didn't argue with people because I had self-control, but I didn't tolerate disrespect. Letting anything, or anyone take me out of character was entirely out of the question.

As I was walking away, I felt the back of my shirt and hair get wet. Turning around, I saw that Sasha was holding an empty glass in her hand with a smirk that I wanted to slap off. Ace stood there frozen with a look of shock plastered on his face. My jaw clenched as I balled up my fists. I started to take a step towards her but stopped myself. She wasn't worth it. The whole situation wasn't worth it. Instead, I turned back around leaving them there to argue amongst themselves as walked out the door.

That was one of the reasons why I didn't go looking for love. Being vulnerable wasn't worth the drama. Before Sasha showed up, I thought Ace might have been worth me putting my heart on the line. I was willing to sacrifice her for a chance at untainted love. Ace made me feel that he had the ability to give that to me. To her. Sasha disrupting our lunch quickly wiped those thoughts away.

🕸️

IT WAS SIX IN THE EVENING, AND I WAS SITTING ON THE couch with the TV on unable to pay attention to a movie that was playing. I hadn't heard from Mr. Baptiste about the job yet, and it was beginning to stress me out.

On top of that, Ace kept invading my thoughts. His voice, how he made me feel, our vibe but most importantly the situation he put me in. He and I weren't dating, we weren't anything, yet water was thrown on me by a woman that he claimed was his ex. Not to mention she claimed to perform oral sex for him the same day he invited me to lunch. I shook my head at the events that had transpired earlier that day. My feelings were all over the place because deep down a part of me wanted to discover more of him and of us.

My phone started to vibrate, and I almost fell off the couch getting up to reach for it from the small cherry wood coffee table that it was on. It was Saint Baptiste. I quickly answered the phone, "Hello."

"Ms. Thomas?"

"This is she."

"How are you doing today? Well, I hope."

"Now that I have received your call, I'm doing very well," I stated.

His laugh was almost inaudible, and then he said, "That's good to hear. I'll keep this short. I'd like to offer you a position. You surprisingly did exceed my expectations. The kitchen staff and servers loved you, and that speaks volumes to me."

I laid the phone back on the coffee table, I put it on speaker, and commenced to jump up and down. Tears of joy began to run down my face.

"However, you won't be able to start this Monday. I need you to come on Tuesday at nine in the morning. We'll go over your contract and then you'll get your official start date."

Making no effort to wipe my tears, I picked up my phone, "Thank you so much for the opportunity. I'll see you on Tuesday."

"Alright, bye Ms. Thomas."

"Bye Mr. Baptiste."

After I hung up the phone, the first thing I wanted to do was share the news with Ace. He had taken a genuine interest in my goals more than anyone I ever met. But telling him about my offer wasn't going to happen. I didn't have his number, and after what happened today, I wasn't sure I wanted it. Since I couldn't tell Ace, I did the next best thing. I picked my phone back up and called my best friend back in Michigan, Chasity.

❦ 6 ❦

Ace

It was Monday morning, and I had been staying at my brother's house in Coral Gables to avoid Sasha. She was most likely going to show up at my condo, and I didn't want to deal with her. She had constantly been calling and texting my phone after our verbal altercation that I ended up blocking her number. If Sasha didn't know I was done with her then, she shouldn't have any doubts now. Seeing her show up at Gayou's, I wasn't really surprised. She knew I ate lunch there often and it was within her character to pop up on me. What did surprise me was her throwing the water on Ladi while she was walking away.

Ladi didn't give Sasha the reaction she was hoping for. She just left which led me to gain a new level of respect for her. Not a lot of women would've been the bigger person. Unlike Ladi, both women that I dealt with after Sasha engaged in the crazy and tried to fight her. Ladi proved that she was the peace that I had been wanting. The peace that

40

would finally put my soul at ease after years of dealing with Sasha's mayhem.

The reason I froze was because she didn't react like I expected her to. Her level of maturity allowed her to walk away and that made me admire her more. She understood that every action didn't deserve a reaction; not many people did.

Di allowed me to be a man by letting me handle the situation, but I failed her. Sasha was going to cause me to lose Ladi before I could actually act on what I felt for her. When I saw her take the money out of her wallet, my pride was shattered. It was beyond a want; I needed to be her protector and provider. I needed to build on what I knew we both felt. Unfortunately, I was failing before I could even start.

All I wanted to do was find a way to see her, apologize, and make her mine. Talking to Saint was my only option, but I didn't feel comfortable enough. He had warned me to stay away from her. I couldn't even fault him because Sasha did exactly what Saint said she would do.

Ladi didn't know Saint, and I were brothers. Through conversation, I could already tell she wouldn't have given me a chance if she knew. Withholding that information, for the time being, was the best option. The other thing was, Saint wouldn't be able to understand what I was feeling. I didn't know how to explain to him what I felt the first night I laid eyes on her.

How could I explain to him that she was my peace, my Ladi? That she was my sole purpose for wanting to chase the possibility of love again. He couldn't understand because I didn't fully understand it.

As if he sensed I needed to talk to him, he opened the door to the guest bedroom that I was staying in. "Bro you have been in this room stinking for a good three days now. What is wrong with you?" After a few seconds, he started laughing. Saint swore he was the funniest person alive.

"Shut up man. I need you to be serious for a minute."

Concern appeared in his eyes, and he became serious, "Talk to me, little bro." He walked inside and sat down on the edge of the bed next to me.

"I messed up Saint."

"How?" he asked.

"Di."

He went from being concerned to confused, "Who is Di?"

"Ladi."

"My manager, Ladi?" he asked, and I felt myself getting frustrated.

He knew exactly who I was referring to. How many women named Ladi could he have possibly known? I sighed and nodded my head. Saint's body language changed, showing that he was angry. He put his face into the palms of his hands in an attempt to control his breathing.

"You decided to hire her permanently?" I asked attempting to change the subject.

He removed his face from his hands and lost it, "Ace I told you I was going to hire her! Just like I told your ass to leave that girl alone! I already knew you being in your feelings had to do with crazy ass, Sasha!"

I sat there quiet as Saint stood up to face me, "Talk before I beat your dumbass."

Being that I was in the wrong, I let him take his anger out on me. Saint was the only person I allowed to talk to me with any form of disrespect. Six years my senior, he always looked out for me. He moved from Saint Lucia with my parents when he was five, whilst I was born in Tennessee.

What my parents couldn't do, Saint did. He hustled so I wouldn't. He struggled, so I didn't have to. The respect I had for him was the reason why I felt like shit for what I was about to tell him.

"I invited Di to lunch after seeing her car at Zubi Supermarket. We were having a great time. We really connected Saint. She's literally everything I needed but was never able to find. Then Sasha showed up and messed it all up. Ladi let me handle the situation but ended up walking away. Next thing I know, Sasha throws water at Ladi while her back was turned. I froze. I fucking froze Saint."

I rubbed my hand down my face. Beyond frustrated with myself, I threw my hands up and hurled myself back onto the bed while still sitting at the edge. "And all Di did was turn around to look at Sasha and left bro! She walked away Saint!" I yelled.

"Did you beat her ass?" he asked.

"Man, what?"

"You heard me Ace. Did...you...beat...Sasha's...ass?" he asked, putting emphasis on each word.

I shook my head, "I'm not putting my hands on a female."

"Ok, but you should've at least choked her," Saint said turning back to his regular self and started laughing. I shook my head and joined him in laughter at his joke. Saint didn't believe in physically harming a woman, but the hatred he had for Sasha made him say off the wall stuff.

"Look Ace; you know what Sasha is capable of. You chose to continue to give that conniving girl attention. That's where you messed up at."

Sitting up I said, "I know, but I did like you told me to. She came over unannounced Saturday morning, and I cut her off completely. I broke things all the way down for her.

We both know I had never done that before. I knew I needed to because I want to pursue Ladi wholeheartedly. Want to know what's crazy?"

He answered, "What?"

"A few hours after I did it, I ran into Di. It was fate man."

Everything flowed the way it was meant to with Ladi. She was beauty in its truest form, beauty in all forms. When she told me that the only love she had experienced was her aunt's, I had already made a promise to myself to give her all the love I had to offer. Even if giving her my love took away from the love I had for myself, I was going to do it.

Saint stood there looking at me and shook his head, "You're dumb. You know that, right?"

"Saint come on. I'm serious." I said.

"So am I. You know that right?" he asked with a smile. I gave in to what he wanted and nodded my head yes.

"As long as you know," he said laughing. "But on a serious tip, if you feel that strongly about Ladi, I'm not going to block you. Love is important Ace. If you feel you can have that with her who am I to stop you? Do what you have to. Just don't let it mess up my business."

"Can you give me her phone number?" I asked while damn near pleading with my eyes.

"Wash your ass, and I got you." And in true Saint fashion, he walked out of the room laughing before closing the door behind him.

I got out of bed and walked into the bathroom to prepare for the day. Whatever it took, I had to get Ladi to give me a fair chance.

Sitting on the couch in Saint's all white living room, I stared at my phone contemplating if I should text or call Ladi.

"You were damn near crying for her number, now you scared to use it," Saint said walking into the living room carrying two short glasses and a bottle of Hennessy.

"She doesn't know we're brothers. I can't tell her you gave me her number." I grabbed the bottle of Hennessy and one of the glasses from him as he sat next to me.

"You better not spill anything on my white couch or white carpet. Wifey would lose her mind if she knew we were drinking in here."

"This the only place we ever drink."

"I know that, but she doesn't." He let out a light chuckle, and I shook my head at him. "But for real, just text her Ace. You're a grown ass man. What do you have to be nervous about?"

"What if she doesn't want to deal with me because she's working for you?"

"If she doesn't want to deal with you it's going to be based on that shit you got going on with Sasha."

"I told you that I completely ended it with Sasha," I said through gritted teeth feeling myself getting irritated.

The Sasha situation was my biggest problem, but I couldn't deny that her working for my brother could pose a threat as well. Ladi was invested in her career and had worked hard to get to where she was. It could easily be rumored that I was the reason she got the position. With that possibility, she wouldn't want to deal with me. There wouldn't be any truth to it, but her reputation would be ruined. I needed to get her to see me first, and then I would let her know I was Saint's younger brother. There were a few things that I wanted to be sure of first before telling her.

"Ladi is the one you need to be explaining that to, not me. Calm your ass down." Saint stated breaking me out of my thoughts.

"I'll handle it."

Deciding to call Ladi, I poured a shot and threw it back. I stood up and walked through the kitchen into the back yard. As I dialed Ladi's number, my heart started to beat faster and faster. The phone rang a couple of times, and then my heart stopped.

She answered, "Hello?" Her sweet voice alone put me in a euphoric state, and I wanted to enjoy every second of it.

"Ladi!" Saying her name, I could feel my heartbeat returning to normal.

Silence. "Talk to me, mama."

"Ace, how did you get my number?"

The fact that she recognized my voice cleared my mind of all negative thoughts. It was something I was experiencing for the first time. If this is what her voice did to me, I could only imagine what her body and love would do.

Ignoring her question, I said everything I had to say, "Di, I am beyond sorry for what happened on Saturday. I've been thinking about you nonstop since then. Let me explain everything to you. Let me meet you somewhere please."

"Ace you don't owe me an explanation." Sadness manifested in her tone.

"Please Di; I want to give you one. Can I meet you somewhere? Anywhere?"

Ladi didn't respond, and if I had to beg her, I was ready. Losing her before I had her, wasn't an option. I refused. "Please Di, I'm begging you." I pleaded with her.

"Little Haiti Soccer Park in an hour."

"Thank you. I'll see you in an hour."

Before I could say anything else, she hung up. Hearing

her agree to meet me, I was over the moon. I walked back inside, and Saint was standing in the kitchen talking to his wife, Angel. Angel was curvy at a size sixteen, and Saint adored every inch of her, from her pecan colored skin to her short light brown pixie cut. She stood at about five feet six to Saint's five feet eleven. They were the epitome of opposites attracting.

Saint was seven years older than Angel. He and Angel started dating when she was eighteen while he was twenty-five. They met while Saint was in Tennessee visiting our parents. The age difference didn't matter to either one because the connection they shared was powerful. Within three months of dating, Saint moved her to Florida, and they've been together ever since. Angel balanced my brother out well. Saint found in Angel what my father found in my mom. When I laid my eyes on Ladi for the first time, I hoped that was the balance I needed.

"What has you smiling so big Ace?" Angel asked.

I shook my head, "Nothing but I have to head out and meet someone. I'll be back later."

"Stop!" Saint yelled. "Pay Ace no mind babe. He knows who has him smiling like that." He had a big grin that caused the smile on my face to grow wider. Waving Saint off, I made my way upstairs to the guest bedroom to prepare for my meeting Ladi. I also had a couple of business

❧ 7 ☙

Ladi

THE LAST THING I WAS EXPECTING TO HAPPEN THIS morning was a phone call from Ace. That call left me feeling a few different things. I was relieved to hear his voice because he had been on my mind constantly since Saturday. Confused because of how strongly he wanted to explain himself. So here I was sitting in the picnic area of the Little Haiti Soccer Park at eleven in the morning waiting on him to explain himself. I wanted an explanation, but I didn't have the right to ask for one. That just wasn't my place no matter what I was feeling for Ace.

I watched as Ace strolled towards me, he was a masterpiece. He had his dreads down to the middle of his back. His beard was full and nicely trimmed. Ace wore burgundy tailored pants, tan loafers, and a white short-sleeve button down. His tall and broad stature looked godly. I wondered if he ever wore lounging clothes. Every time I saw him, he was dressed up. I was wearing a sports bra and compression leggings because I planned on going for a run after our talk. As soon as he reached me, I stood up to greet him. He had a small gift bag and flowers in his hand.

"Beauty, these are for you." He handed me a dozen lavender roses.

It was charming that he was using his words to be affectionate knowing how I felt about the power that words held. "Thank you; I've never seen lavender roses before." I took them from him, gave him a quick hug, and sat back down.

Still holding the gift bag in his hand, he sat down next to me and said, "Lavender roses represent love at first sight and enchantment."

He smiled, and I could feel the heat in my body rising. He then turned to face me as he put his hand on my thigh like he did at Gayou's. "Let me start by saying I'm sorry. Putting you in a position like that was never my intention."

The sincerity in his voice and eyes made my heart believe him immediately. I nodded, and he continued, "Sasha and I broke up a year ago. Every attempt I made to move on from her she ruined. To be real, I allowed her to. I kept her around because none of the women seemed to be worth the trouble she brought. Sasha shouldn't have had that much power, but I am man enough to say that I gave it to her. It wasn't until I laid eyes on you, did I want to deal with the trouble she brought."

His words seemed earnest, but I wasn't sure if I wanted to deal with the troubles that he and his situation would bring. However, denying our connection was something I couldn't do. Still, after the argument he had with his ex, I wondered if it was worth it. Sitting there silently, I allowed him to get everything off his chest.

"Beauty what she said wasn't all true, I need you to know that. As soon as I saw you in the parking lot, I made the decision to cut her off entirely to focus on pursuing you. She came over unannounced Saturday morning, and I told her that she and I were completely done. I didn't tell her about you, but I did tell her the truth. The truth is, love is something I want Di, and that's what I told her. Sasha cannot give me that nor do I want it from her. Then she was on her knees with my manhood in her mouth. I stopped her as soon as I was able to process everything. She and I haven't had sex in six months."

"Ace, you really don't have to explain yourself." I finally said to him.

"But I do, Di. I want you, but most importantly, I want you to give me a chance Beauty."

I sat there stuck after his proclamation. It was what I wanted to hear, but I wasn't sure if I was ready for it. Because Ace poured out everything he felt to me, it was only right I did the same. Yet, I couldn't. Not this soon. Though, I had to let him know what took place on Saturday afternoon could not happen again. "I want to give you a chance Ace, but I refuse to be disrespected by your ex."

The smirk that spread across his face was infectious, and I began to smile. He moved closer, and I could feel myself melting into him. My goals the past few years of my life had been school and my career. Now that I received my master's and had gotten my dream position at Chez Saint, maybe now was the perfect time to take a chance at love. Love happened when it was meant to happen. My heart felt like it was happening now, and she wouldn't allow me to run away from it even if I wanted to. Thankfully, I didn't.

I wasn't sure if I would've felt that way if it were any other man besides Ace. He made me want to take a chance with him, at love. The few men that I dated in the past didn't do that. That was the main reason why I was still single.

"Don't worry about that Di; I handled it. I swear you just made me the happiest man Beauty. I got you something else."

Ace handed me the gift bag that had been in his hand the entire time. He had the silliest smirk, and I laughed on the inside at how excited he was. I took the bag from him and opened it. Seeing the contents of the bag caused my mouth to fall open and my eyes to water. I looked back up at him, and his smile was still stretched across his face.

I was speechless as I removed three envelopes which I was sure had greeting cards in them along with a Pandora box. I laid the cards on my lap to open the box. It held a silver bracelet with three charms on it.

"One charm for each day that has passed since I've met you. That bracelet will represent everything that I am willing to offer you if you are willing to have me uncondi-tionally Beauty. These are the Pandora Essence loyalty charm, friendship charm, and the caring charm. The more I get to know you, the more charms I plan to add."

After he said all of that, how could I not start giving myself to this man? He understood me and regardless of my reservations, he was willing to put the effort to get rid of them. I made the decision not to fight what I felt when our eyes first connected and take in all that he was willing to offer.

Ace reached over and took the bracelet out of the box. As he put the bracelet on my left wrist, he purposely rubbed his fingers against my skin. Ace bent down and kissed my forehead. I closed my eyes hoping to enjoy the moment for as long as I could. As if closing my eyes could preserve the warmth that he brought me — his soft kiss representing the love that I was praying that we would grow into. Ace removed his lips from my forehead forcing me to open my eyes.

"Thank you, Ace. All of this is too much."

"Ladi, nothing I ever do for you will be too much. You understand me?"

I smiled at him and responded, "Yes, I understand."

"One last thing and we're done talking about what happened on Saturday."

I nodded my head waiting for him to continue. To my knowledge, there wasn't anything else that had to be said. He apologized and explained the situation with his ex. I had never been one to dwell on the past.

"That sixty dollars you left on the table, I left there as a tip for the waitress. Please don't disrespect me like that again. I told you once, and this is my second time, don't let there be a third Di. You were being petty. I'm going to let it slide because I was in the wrong. Just make sure it doesn't happen again."

I looked down at the ground making sure to avoid eye contact with him. It was my way of telling him that I didn't need him. What I wasn't expecting was to be sitting next to him two days later willing to give him a chance to explore what we both felt. "It won't happen again Ace. I promise." I responded.

I leaned over bumping my shoulder to his arm to lighten the mood. He looked down at me as he shook his head. My bump didn't cause him to move an inch. After a few minutes of small talk, I shared the news of my position at Chez Saint. He was just as excited as I was.

We sat and continued talking for a little while longer until it was time for him to head to his meeting. "I'm going to go on my run. I'm not sure why you won't tell me how you got my number, but since I have your number, I'll call you when I get done." I said.

"Let me take you out tonight Beauty. We can redo our first date."

I looked at his face to see if he was serious. He was very serious. Since I agreed to give him a chance, I agreed to the redo date. We both stood and walked towards the parking lot. He walked me to my car to put the gift bag and flowers in it. When we reached my car, I put them inside and turned back around.

"Come here." Ace pulled me closer to him and wrapped his arm around my waist. I laid my head on his chest, enjoying the moment with him. It was then that I wished I could've stayed in his arms forever. Unwilling to pull myself away, I sunk deeper into Ace. He must've felt my body relaxing at his embrace because he drew me in even closer. The feeling was foreign to me, yet Ace felt like familiarity. After a few more seconds had passed, Ace pulled away still holding on to my waist.

"Go ahead and go on your run Beauty. Call or text me when you get home."

"Why do you call me beauty?" Him calling me Di made sense to me, but beauty didn't. I had been dying to ask, but we had more important things to discuss

"You are beauty in its purest form."

His answer completely caught me off guard. Don't get me wrong, I fully embraced my natural beauty. It was just that, that wasn't the response that I expected from him. Ace spoke without thinking. He didn't process his reasoning before speaking which made his words honest. Unfiltered.

He continued, "Your hair, your skin, your poise, your body. Everything about you physically is pure. Your ambition is what attracts me to you the most. I see us growing in love together. A pure and infinite love. An untainted love."

The only thing I could do was nod my head, "I understand. I'll call you later, ok." Ace leaned down and kissed my forehead again. His lips against my skin made me weak. I couldn't help but imagine how his lips would feel against mine. We said our goodbyes and Ace turned around to walk to his car. I observed him walk away wondering how his presence could give me strength whereas leaving made me weak.

❦ 8 ❦

Ladi

When I returned from my run, my aunt's car wasn't outside. That's how it had been for as long as I could remember. My aunt was always working over-time. She worked a lot over the years to prevent me from taking out an overwhelming amount of student loans. Working part-time as a waitress all six years that I was in school reduced the amount of help that I needed for neces-sities and my car note. I was hoping that in a few months I could convince her to only work part-time because she would never quit her job.

Getting out of my car, I walked towards the small two-bedroom home that my aunt raised me in. All my dreams of paying her mortgage off would happen soon enough. My aunt was happy living in Little Haiti, and I was not going to take away her happiness. She took me in at two years old and raised me as if I were her own while never letting me forget my parents. I was grateful for everything she had done for me.

The second I made it through the door, my phone

began vibrating. It was my best friend, Chasity, calling. I hurried in, sat on the couch, and answered the phone, "Hey Chas!"

"Ladi! I'm moving back to Miami. I can't do Michigan anymore."

"What happened?" I asked.

Chasity and I met my last year at Florida International University. She was a junior, and I was a senior. We instantly clicked, later became best friends. Once I was accepted into Michigan State University, she decided to transfer with me and complete her last year of undergraduate there. Talking Chasity out of moving proved pointless because she was headstrong. When her mind was made up, it was made up.

When we moved to Michigan, I pursued my masters whereas Chasity chose to not continue with school. Instead, she became a bottle girl and a video model for a few local rappers. I couldn't knock her hustle since she hustled for everything she had. Chasity never asked anyone for help, and she did whatever she had to do to survive. I respected her for it. To hear that she was moving back to Miami was shocking for a few reasons. One being that when I brought up moving back to Miami, she told me that she would never come back.

"Kenny! I swear I'm over him! He has babies on the way!" She yelled. Chasity was screaming so loud that I had to remove the phone from my ear. I put the phone on speaker and sat it on the coffee table.

"Babies?" I asked

"B-A-B-I-E-S. As in more than one!" If I hadn't heard the hurt and anger in her voice, I would've laughed. Chasity was always animated which was why she spelled out babies.

"Wow!"

Kenny was a grimy type of guy through and through. My best friend was brokenhearted over a man that wasn't even worthy of her. She wanted hood love, but her ideal hood love was missing one thing, the right man. She never fell for the romantic savage, always the bum.

Chasity had been dating Kenny for four months and although she had multiple warning signs she chose to stay. He constantly disrespected her and cheated on her. At one point in time, he made advances at me. When I told her about it, she refused to believe me. She even threatened to move out of the apartment the two of us shared. It wasn't until he admitted to her that he did it did she believe me. That was the only good thing about him, he was always honest if she asked. Afterward, she didn't apologize, we just both acted like it never happened.

"I hate him! One, I could deal with but two! Two kids with two different women! No, ma'am! They can keep that because I don't want it!"

"I feel you, Chas." I pitied my best friend. Although I had never been in love, I knew enough to know that her past relationships weren't love. They were a convenience for the men and her desperate need to feel love. Chasity was beautiful. She was mixed with black and white but mainly had black features. She had green eyes and was two inches taller than me at five feet five. She had a body that was similar to Porsha from the Real Housewives of Atlanta. Her looks were one of her many qualities, but she always chose to waste her time on men that weren't deserving.

"I'm coming back in three weeks, I just have to finish up a couple of music videos first. Do you think your aunt will let me stay there until I get approved for an apartment?"

My aunt was used to Chas staying over so I knew she wouldn't mind especially since it was temporary. As much as my aunt worked, she probably wouldn't even notice her being there. "I'm sure she will, but I will talk to her when she gets home," I answered.

As soon as I said that, I heard my aunt unlocking the front door. "Chas, my aunt just walked in. Let me talk to her, and I'll call you back."

"Ok. Call me back so I can finish telling you about bionic sperm boy."

We laughed before I promised to call her back. As I looked over at my aunt, I noticed that her eyes were low, and she looked fatigued. I couldn't wait to start at Chez Saint in order to help her more. I had three thousand saved up from waitressing, but it wasn't enough to stop her from working as much as she did. "Stop looking at me like that Ladi. I only went in for a five-hour shift."

"I can't help it, Auntie Marie. You work too hard."

"No such thing as working too hard cherie." Her calling me darling in Haitian Creole was her way of letting me know she no longer wanted to discuss the subject. It softened me every time. My aunt made sure I spoke Creole fluently. The pride she had in her Haitian culture was passed down to me. Although my father was American, I never knew him or his side of the family. Therefore, I felt like I was fully Haitian. "Ok, Auntie but I have something I need to ask you."

She was still standing at the door. She sat her bags by the door, took her shoes off, and walked over to me. Sitting next to me on the couch, she threw her head back in exhaustion. I ignored my urge to say something about her working too hard again.

"Chas just called to tell me that she's moving back to Miami in three weeks. She wanted me to ask you if she could stay here until she got approved for her apartment."

My aunt looked at me and said, "You know I don't mind her staying here. But you're my niece, and I want you to be careful with her."

My aunt loved Chasity, but she didn't trust her after I told her about how Chasity reacted to me telling her about Kenny's advances. I was hurt, and I needed to talk it out with someone. The only person that I had to talk through it with was my aunt. It didn't occur to me that her views on Chasity would change until after the fact. "I hear you, Auntie."

"Kreyol pale, Kreyol konprann cherie." She ended the conversation with the Haitian Creole proverb that translated to Creole is spoken, Creole is understood. Meaning, what was understood didn't need to be explained.

Auntie Marie stood up and walked towards the back of the house to her room. She was most likely going to try to get some rest before work later that night. Raising up from the couch, I grabbed my phone and headed to the bathroom to take a shower. Before getting in, I sent Ace a text.

Me: Ace, I made it made home. Let me know where to meet you for our date tonight."

I took off my Nikes, sports bra, and compression leggings and got in the shower. The hot water poured on my skin as I reminisced on the time that Ace and spent together.

STEPPING OUT THE SHOWER, I TOOK MY TOWEL OFF THE rack and wrapped it around my body. I grabbed my phone and noticed a text from Ace.

Ace: Beauty you're going to stop playing with me. Send

me your address for me to come pick you up at six. Dress up.

Ace picking me up meant I had to tell my aunt about him. My aunt begged me every day to start taking dating seriously because she didn't want me to be lonely. She always praised me for my work ethic which I got from her. But in the same breath, she would condemn me for never putting myself out there to seek a man. Now I wasn't left with a choice but to tell her.

I gathered my things from the bathroom and made my way to my aunt's room that was directly beside mine further down the hallway. Once I made it to her door, I knocked on it twice.

"Come in Ladi!" she yelled.

I opened the door and walked in leaving the door open behind me. "Auntie Marie, I have a friend that is going to pick me up at six to go out. I know you'll want to meet him."

Although my aunt spent most of her life in America, she held on to many of her Haitian customs. If a man was going to be at her doorstep for me, she was going to have to meet him and talk to him. She rose from the bed as a pool of tears threatened to fall from her eyes, "Cherie, you make auntie so happy."

I couldn't help but laugh at how dramatic my aunt was acting. She had been pressuring me for the past two years to get serious about a guy. I tried to do it, but the few attempts I made didn't go well. It was easier to put all my effort into school than to be disappointed by them. With Ace, it felt different. I didn't think I would be disappointed no matter how far it went.

"Very funny Auntie. I'm going to get started on my hair because I only have about four hours to get ready."

"Ok, cherie. Let me know when he gets here."

"Yes, ma'am."

Once in my room, I quickly sent Ace a text so that I could get started on my hair.

Me: I wasn't trying to play with you, I was trying to save you lol. 7200 NW Miami Place 33150. My aunt is excited to meet you

He replied immediately.

Ace: Not having you is the only thing that can scare me Beauty. See you soon

He knew all the right things to say. Instead of replying to him, I went and plugged in my flat iron.

❦

IT WAS 5:45 PM AS I LOOKED AT MYSELF IN THE FULL-length mirror that hung on the back of my bedroom door. My flat ironed hair with added loose curls hung two inches past my shoulders. An Ankara African print knee length dress I had gotten in the mail last week felt like the perfect dress for our redo date. The fitted gold, red, and black print dress was off the shoulder and hugged my curves perfectly. I matched it with red open-toed sandal heels. My bright red lip stain paired perfectly with my milk chocolate complexion.

After looking over myself in the mirror for a few minutes, I went to the living room to wait for Ace. My aunt was sitting on the couch already waiting for him. The way she stared at me, you would've thought I was about to go to my senior prom. "You are beautiful cherie."

"Thank you. I hoped I'm dressed appropriately." I twirled around so that my aunt could see the back of my dress as well.

"I think you are dressed to go anywhere."

I was still standing up talking to my aunt when I heard a knock at the door. Ace was earlier than six o'clock which I knew my aunt would appreciate. Before I could make my way to the door, Auntie Marie was up and opening the door for Ace.

The minute the door opened I wished I had my phone in hand so that I could've recorded Ace's reaction. His mouth dropped open, and his eyes popped out at the sight of me. He was wearing a dark gray tailored dress pant and matching jacket. His white dress shirt and tan oxfords were the perfect contrast to his dark skin. His hair was back up in the same updo he had when I saw him at Zubi's. His cologne assaulted my nose as soon as my aunt opened the door. He smelled amazing. He always smelled amazing.

I didn't know if it was the dress or my hair, but he couldn't take his eyes off of me. My aunt looked back and forth at us waiting for Ace to speak, but he stood there just gazing at me. It was crazy that this man that left me speechless with his presence every time and was now speechless at the mere sight of me.

❦ 9 ❦

Ace

Damn! That's the only word that came to mind. Hands down, Ladi was the most beautiful woman I had ever met. The way the African print dress wrapped around her body had me imagining how much more beautiful she would be with it off. My eyes roamed her body finally stopping at her lips. She wasn't leaving me tonight without me tasting them.

"Are you going to keep staring at my niece or you going to come in and speak?" To the left of me stood who I assumed to be her aunt. It came off as rude not to speak, but Ladi left me in a daze. In four days I felt like I saw her in every form — professional, relaxed, athletic, and now this.

"I apologize ma'am. I was admiring Ladi's beauty."

"I see. Call me Auntie Marie. You can come in and have a seat." She said while pointing at the tan love seat.

63

When I initially told Ladi I was picking her up; I didn't think that I would've had to meet nor talk to her aunt. But if that's what I had to do to get a redo date with Ladi, then I was more than willing to do it. Her aunt played an important role in who she was today and that alone, made me feel privileged to meet her. I walked over to the love seat to take my seat. Ladi was still standing, and for the first time since I had met her, she looked nervous.

"Ladi go sit next to him cherie." Aunt Marie said. Aunt Marie had me loving her already. She didn't know the happiness she brought to my heart by telling Ladi to come sit next to me. Since I first laid eyes on Ladi, I always wanted her around me. It may sound foolish, but I was ready for her to move in with me so that I could wake up to her every morning. It was too soon, but that's how she had me feeling.

Ladi walked over to me, and again I was in a daze. Perfection doesn't exist, but Ladi was the closest thing to it. She sat down next to me making sure to leave three inches of space between us. I desperately wanted to close it, but out of respect for her aunt, I fought the desire. Hearing her aunt's voice brought me out of my trance.

"Young man, Ladi is a good girl. She's very smart and a very hard worker. I want her to have a good man. If you are not a good man, leave her alone."

The thing was, I didn't just want to be a good man; my goal was to be Ladi's man. Everything she said about Ladi was true, and that's why in my soul I knew that Ladi was my ideal woman. Looking over at Ladi before responding to Auntie Marie, I had to take in this woman one last time before I spoke the words that were dying to leave my lips. Her hands were sitting on her lap allowing me to notice that she was still wearing the Pandora bracelet I had given to her. The bracelet being on her arm was the reassurance I needed.

"Auntie Marie, you don't have to worry about anything negative happening to Ladi's mind, body, heart, or spirit. My goal is to cultivate her and help her reach her full potential in everything she does."

She looked at Ladi with a straight face and said, "I like him Ladi." Auntie Marie looked back at me, "Make sure she enjoys herself tonight because she starts her new job tomorrow."

Her aunt mentioning that she had gotten the job reminded me that I had to find a way to tell her that Saint was my brother. The timing was the only problem. If I told her now, I knew she wouldn't take the chance of ruining her credibility. She would end us before we ever really began. Telling her too late would blow up in my face as well which meant I had to time it perfectly. Either way, losing Ladi wasn't an option for me.

"We are definitely going to celebrate that tonight," I said as I looked over at Ladi. She was quiet the whole time and kept fidgeting with her two pointer fingers. Because I could tell she was getting antsy, I made the decision that it was time for us to leave.

"We have reservations at 7:30 and I don't want us to be late. It was nice meeting you, and I'm looking forward to seeing you again Auntie Marie."

I stood up while reaching for Ladi's hand to help her stand as well. Aunt Marie walked us to the door and gave us both hugs. After I pulled away from her embrace, I noticed how much Di favored her. I was completely focused on Ladi that I hadn't really taken the chance to look at her aunt. Anyone could've mistaken Di for her daughter.

I led Ladi out the door to my car by the small of her

back. Walking her over to the passenger side, I opened the door for her. Once she was seated, I closed the door and walk over to the driver side. I got in, backed out of the driveway, and headed to South Beach.

"So where are you taking me for our redo date?" Di asked soon after I pulled out of the driveway.

"I almost thought you forgot how to speak Beauty. You were quiet the whole time I was speaking with your aunt." I smiled at her hoping that she would smile back. For the first time, I wasn't purposely avoiding her question. Normally, I evaded her questions in the past because I liked to lead the conversation. But I genuinely wanted to know where her head was at.

"You are the first man that showed interest in me that I chose to introduce to my aunt." She said looking down almost as if she was embarrassed.

"Hold your head up Beauty." I glanced over at her for a few seconds to make sure she held her head up before I continued, "Talk to me, mama."

"The guys I dated in the past weren't that serious..."

I cut her off "And we are serious." It was more a statement than a question, but she didn't catch on.

"No, that's not what I'm saying." She sighed, "It's the way my aunt reacted with you. I can tell she likes you. Then what you said about wanting to help me reach my full potential. I guess I was taking my time to process it all."

I nodded my head as she spoke. Taking another glance at her, I noticed she was playing with the Pandora bracelet on her wrist. In a weird way, I understood where she was coming from. Although I had dated other women in the past, it felt different with Ladi. In a very short amount of time, we had a connection that was indescribable. She was new to me, but she felt right.

"I meant every word Beauty. I like your vibe when we're together, I admire your drive and professionalism, I adore your full lips and almond-shaped eyes, and I appreciate your time."

"I like your vibe, I admire your persistence, I adore your dark skin and full beard, and I appreciate the effort you're putting forth Ace."

Damn! Could this girl draw me in anymore? Never had a woman took the time to point out specific things that she liked about me. I was beginning to understand why Ladi put as much importance on words as she did. She couldn't physically touch my heart or soul, but her words did easily. "You are beautiful in every sense of the word. Pure, genuine, and real, all of the above Di."

"Thank you. So where are we going for our redo date?"

After a light chuckle, I answered, "We're having dinner at Juvia. I figured you would like the space and afterward a walk."

Juvia was a restaurant that was on top of a parking garage. It was modern and had a beautiful view of South Beach. I felt that Ladi would really appreciate the space. I wanted to do something romantic but simple for our redo date. With her just moving back to Miami, I figured that it would be perfect.

"Are you serious?" I looked over as her eyes lit up. "I've been dying to go there." I made the right choice. Juvia had an Asian, Peruvian, and French menu. With food and restaurant management being her passion, I knew she would enjoy it. The first date was casual and random. The fact that she appreciated it made me want to go all out for this one.

As we got closer to our destination, I said, "I'm going to park in a garage nearby, and we're going to walk to Juvia. I know you're wearing heels, so I can carry you if you'd like."

She laughed, but I was serious. "I wouldn't wear them if I couldn't walk in them."

She had a point, which meant I didn't have a smart comeback for her. I nodded my head and joined her in laughter. We had finally made it to the parking garage, and I hurried to get out of the car. I swiftly walked over to Ladi's door before she could open it. She was looking up at me like I was crazy, but I knew what I was doing. Opening her door, I watched her unbuckle her seatbelt. As soon as she was unbuckled, I pulled her from the seat and into my chest.

I wasn't trying to mess up her hair, but I needed her in my arms. I needed her there as soon as I had first laid eyes on her tonight but hadn't had the opportunity. She melted in my arms, and I could feel her body relax with each breath she took. It was as if her skin began to literally dissolve into mine. I no longer belonged to myself; I belonged to her and her only.

"You look so fucking beautiful Beauty." I had been waiting to say that all night because I needed her to be in my arms when I told her.

"Thank you, Ace." She replied softly.

I closed my eyes hoping to fall deeper into the moment, "Ladi, what do I have to do to make you mine?"

The question must've taken her off guard because she pulled back a little to look up at me causing me to open my eyes. "Give me time. In my heart, I know I'm yours. I just need time to physically become yours."

I drew her back in before closing my eyes. She felt exactly how I felt, and I couldn't help but be appreciative. It would make our journey together more peaceful. I couldn't ruin this moment by telling her Saint was my older brother.

I couldn't risk losing her knowing she felt how I felt. Against my better judgment, I chose to withhold it from her for tonight. Tonight just wasn't the right time. "Anything you need, know that I got you. Let's go enjoy our redo date Beauty." Reluctantly letting her go, I took her right hand into my left.

As I walked with her, I took the time to appreciate her natural beauty. Her hair was beautiful. Her lips were full, the perfect size. Her beauty unmeasured. I was a foot taller than Ladi, and it gave me comfort. In a way, it made me feel more like her protector. I loved that her body wasn't exaggerated like some of the women in Miami. Her breasts were small but enough. Her hips were naturally wide, and her thighs and ass matched perfectly. I had noticed her body before now, but tonight I took my time to really admire it. If I had any doubts before, tonight I didn't. Tonight proved without a doubt that our connection went beyond the physical; it was a connection of souls.

When we made it to the rooftop of the garage, I could see the excitement in Ladi's eyes. Juvia was the perfect spot to bring her. I had called ahead of time to have them reserve a table for two with a view of South Beach. The hostess walked us back to our table as I kept my eyes on Ladi the entire time.

"AAAACCCCCCEEE!!" she squealed my name once we reached our table.

That was the exact reaction I was hoping for. I had gotten our waiter to put a greeting card, a dozen hot pink roses, and a small Pandora gift bag in the middle of our table. Ladi turned around and hugged me around my waist. These were simple gestures, but with the way she reacted, she would have you think I was giving her the world.

Putting my arm around her waist, I guided her to her

seat. I pulled the seat out for her, waited for her to sit down, and walked around to take my place across from her. She quickly picked up and opened the envelope to pull out the card. She admired the front of the card and went to place it back on the table.

"Read the card."

"I haven't read the other ones," she responded.

"You can read the other ones later. I want you to read this one in front of me, out loud Beauty."

She nodded and began reading, "Beauty, congratulations on your journey to success and the start of your career. You've taken another step towards achieving your dream, and I am honored to be able to witness it. When you reach the last step, I want to be there to witness that as well. So, whenever you are ready, even if it's five years from now, consider this card as an IOU for the design of your restaurant Di."

Ladi looked up at me with widened eyes, "The dark pink roses mean appreciation and gratitude. I just need you to know that I am grateful that you agreed to this redo date with me."

I reached over to take the gift bag from the table and pulled out the small box, "This charm represents faith, I want you to have faith in me, Beauty. Have faith in all that I have to give you. Faith that I want to be a part of making your dreams our reality." Making it a point to put an emphasis on our.

"I don't know what to say Ace because thank you isn't enough. Your gestures are beyond anything that I could've imagined. The effort that you've put in to this, everything, is the reason I'm not fighting what I feel for you. It's too early to say I'm yours, but I want to get to that point."

Without saying a word, I stood up from my seat, walked

over to her, and pointed to her arm that had the bracelet on it. "Take it off."

She removed the bracelet, and she handed it to me. After taking it from her, I put the faith charm on it and placed it back on her wrist. I wanted to take in everything that I was feeling with Ladi. Once I was back in my seat, we stared into each other's eyes without speaking a word to one another. Ladi wasn't fighting me or playing hard to get. Instead, she appreciated all that I had to offer. With Ladi, it went beyond physical attraction. Our attraction was mental, spiritual, and emotional. A connection like that wasn't something to fight against. Her feeling the same way I felt gave me a purpose. My goal was to give Ladi the love she was in love with but had yet to experience.

Our waiter, a short, middle-aged white male with blond hair, came to the table breaking our silence, "Good evening, my name is Tony. I will be your server tonight. Can I start you all with something to drink?"

I ordered first, "Can I get a bottle of Dom Perignon and two glasses of water? We are celebrating tonight."

"Yes sir, you can. Are you and the lady ready to order now or would you like me to come back?" Tony asked.

I looked over at Ladi and asked, "Would you like me to order for you since this is your first time here?"

"Yes, I love seafood." During our conversation at Gayou's restaurant, I had learned that Ladi's favorite food was seafood.

"I remember Beauty. Trust me, I remember everything you've told me."

I ordered the Australian rack of lambs with Jasmine rice for myself and the diver sea scallop with Jasmine rice for Ladi. After I ordered, we thanked Tony and waited for him to return. Soon after, he returned with two glasses of water, two champagne flutes, and the Dom Perignon. I watched Ladi as she watched him walk away.

"When are you going to tell me your last name?" Ladi asked as soon as the waiter walked

I didn't know how to answer that question. I wasn't ready for Ladi to connect me to Saint just yet. Getting her to fall in love with me was my plan and knowing that I was her boss's younger brother was only going to hinder that. I wasn't willing to take that chance. "When we get married," I answered.

A smiled appeared from her, and she began blushing. Ladi wasn't going to accept that answer, but it felt good knowing that she blushed at the idea of us getting married one day. "Seriously Ace?" She looked at me through her now squinted eyes while folding her arms under her size B breasts.

"As a heart attack. You are going to be my wife one day Beauty." I did mean it, Ladi was going to be my wife one day.

"Well, I need to know your last name before that happens."

"Baptiste."

Her eyes widened, "Any relation to Saint Baptiste?"

Her widened eyes heightened the anxiety that I was already feeling. She knew my last name, but that didn't mean I wanted to tell her I was related to Saint. Not yet, at least. It wasn't that I wanted to be dishonest, I just couldn't allow myself to lose her. I needed a little more time with her then I would tell her. We needed to experience what we were feeling for one another before she found out.

I knew Ladi well enough at this point to know that if a fake rumor went around that I had something to do with her getting the job, she would cut me off. She would only worry about her career, and I couldn't handle that. Now that she had expressed to me how she felt, I wanted to show her that there was room in her life to balance love as well as a successful career.

"Do you know how many people with the last name Baptiste there are in this world?" I asked, avoiding answering her question directly.

"Yes, but I want to make sure."

"Make sure of what?" I asked.

"That you aren't related to him. I am feeling you Ace, but I can't have people credit my accomplishments to any involvement I have with you if you're related to him."

She confirmed what I had already suspected. She would cut me off if she knew I was related to Saint. I wasn't necessarily lying to her, but I wasn't being honest either. I just wanted her to follow her heart and go with the flow with me. She needed to be certain in the future that we could build together and that her dreams were my priority. I was there to nurture them by helping her achieve them. Not being completely honest about my relation to Saint with her was the only way I knew how do that.

I opened the bottle of Dom Perignon and poured some into both flutes. "You don't have to worry about that Ladi."

Putting the bottle down, I reached over to grab her left hand and brought to my lips. I silently prayed that Ladi hadn't caught on to me not answering her questions directly. Leaving her hand in mine, I waited for her to change the subject.

"That's good to know." She responded as she tightened her grip on my hand.

Deep down I felt like shit because it was wrong to lie to her. I just wanted her to give us a chance and not let what others might say cloud her judgment. Because I knew that wasn't going to happen, I did what I thought was best. It wasn't in me to argue that I was in the right when I was obviously in the wrong. I was just hoping that when I told Ladi the truth that she would care more about the reason behind my actions instead of the act itself.

Tony finally returned with our food, "Australian lamb chops and Jasmine rice for you sir. For the lady, we have the diver sea scallop with Jasmine rice."

Tony coming permitted me the opportunity to change the subject without Ladi getting suspicious. I had never been more relieved to see a waiter in my life. "Thank you, Tony." we both said in unison.

We looked at each other, and we both started laughing. Hearing Ladi's laugh did something to me every time. I yearned to have that feeling for the rest of our lives. "Can I get anything else for you all?" Tony asked after we were done laughing.

"Not right now," I replied.

"Ok, sir. You all enjoy your food, and I will be back to check in later."

We thanked Tony one more time before he turned around to leave. I looked back at Ladi and noticed she was staring at her food. "Why are you looking at your food like that?"

"It looks too pretty to eat Ace."

I let out a soft chortle. Never had I heard anyone describe food as too pretty to eat. Taking my phone out of my pocket, I snapped a picture of her staring her plate. She looked up at me confused as my smile stretched wider. "I took a picture for you crazy girl. Now you can eat your food and stop staring at it." I explained.

"Me staring at my food is crazy?" She asked as she crossed her arms underneath her breasts.

That was the second time she did that tonight. It had to be something she did when she was trying to get an attitude. The only thing was, her voice had a sweetness that wouldn't allow me to take any attitude she may have had seriously.

"Yeah because your mouth is watering. Just eat your food."

With her arms still folded she said, "That's exactly how you look at me."

Shrugging my shoulders, I replied, "Feed me then."

As soon as my words escaped my lips, Ladi almost fell out of her seat. She cleared her throat and fixed herself in her sit. I continued, "Just know that still won't ever stop me from staring at you."

"Let's eat our food." She quickly replied.

Was I being forward? Definitely. Still, having a sexual conversation shouldn't have made a twenty-four years old woman as uncomfortable as it made Ladi. She said she wasn't a virgin, which was why I didn't see the issue. Ignoring her reaction, I smiled at her. We began eating our food and continued enjoying each other's company.

❧ 10 ❧

Ace

"Did you enjoy yourself Beauty?" I asked Ladi.

"I really did Ace. That was the most romantic date I've ever been on. You made it a celebration of my hard work and that means the world to me."

We were seated in my car outside of Ladi's house. Dinner went better than I had anticipated. The walk we took afterward allowed us to get more mentally intimate with one another. Now it was one in the morning, but I wasn't ready to let her leave yet. "I'm glad you enjoyed yourself Beauty. What time do you have to be at work in the morning?"

"Nine."

"Are you nervous?"

"Not really, I'm more excited than I am nervous." She replied.

"Understandable. I'll be real with you, I'm not trying to end this date, but I know you need your rest."

"Me either. You can come back over tomorrow night, and I'll make us dinner. How does that sound?" She asked.

"That sounds good to me Beauty. Do you know what time you're getting off? I don't want you to be tired from work and then have to cook."

"I don't know yet, but it doesn't matter. If I'm tired, I'll make sure to let you know."

"Ok. Let's get you inside."

Getting out of the car, I walked over to Ladi's side to help her out as well. I was doing my best to keep my composure, but on the inside, I was losing it. Ladi offering to cook for me was the ultimate test of the type of woman she was. My mom always told me to appreciate a woman that took her time to cook a meal for me. She also explained the difference in the two types of women that offered to cook.

A woman that was cooking for me out of obligation was a woman that expected something in return. If she felt like it was a job or a chore, she expected some type of payment. If the payment she received in return wasn't what she felt she deserved, she would either slack off or quit altogether. I experienced that with Sasha. She was a great cook, but if she didn't get her way, she wouldn't cook for days. That didn't bother me like she thought it would because my mom made sure Saint and I were self-sufficient enough to take care of ourselves. Cooking, cleaning, ironing, our mom made sure we did it all.

The second type of woman cooked because she truly wanted to. She didn't expect anything in return. Even if she was mad or not speaking to me, she would still make sure I had a homecooked meal. My mother taught me that this was the type of woman that not only do I provide for, but I had to serve her as well. Just because she didn't expect anything in return didn't mean appreciation wasn't given to her. My dad did it for my mom, Saint for Angel, and now I desperately wanted to do it for Ladi.

Once we made it to Ladi's front door, I pulled her into me by her waist. Her heels added a few inches, so she was able to drape her arms around the back of my neck with more ease than I expected. I looked down into her eyes, and she looked up at me. My eyes traveled down to her lips, and I knew I couldn't leave without tasting them. Typically, I would just go in for a kiss, but I wanted Di to want it as much as I did. Looking back into her eyes, I searched for any sign of resistance. Unable to find any, I bent down placing my lips on hers.

Her lips were softer than I could've imagined. As soon as I felt her lips part giving me permission to continue, I took her top lip into mine, sucking it as if it would be my only chance to do so. As our kiss grew deeper, I could feel Ladi getting weaker. I held onto her tighter as I moved my tongue inside of her mouth. Her tongue wrapped around mine and I knew at that moment she had just given me herself physically.

Even though I wanted to taste all of her, I pulled away from Ladi as I felt my manhood grow harder. Ladi had already shown me that she was uncomfortable talking about sex. The last thing I wanted to do was make her uneasy by feeling him against her.

Ladi finally opened her eyes. She grabbed by my neck, back down to her lips and whispered, "I'm yours Ace."

That was exactly what I needed to hear before I drew her in even closer and took her lip back into mine. I picked Ladi up and wrapped her legs around my waist. Her knee-length fitted African print dress rose up to the bottom of her ass. Putting her back against her front door, I pushed my pelvis into hers. Although I wasn't going to take it there with her tonight, I wanted her to feel the effect she had on my body. The wetness between her legs seeped through her panties and onto the front of my pants. I wanted to be inside of her, I needed it, but this wasn't the time nor the place. I wanted our first time together to be special. Catering to all her physical needs was a must for me. I wouldn't have been able to right now, so I refrained from taking it further.

Slowly putting Ladi down, I reluctantly separated my lips from hers. If a few minutes of passionate kissing had us like this, I couldn't wait to see what the future held for us. Ladi opened her eyes, and I watched her as she fixed her hair. As she started to fix her dress, her eyes went to bulge in my pants causing her to look up at me.

I gently grabbed her face with both of my hands, "What's wrong Beauty?"

She tried to look down, but I held on to her face, "I'm embarrassed."

I knew that, but I couldn't understand why, "What do you have to be embarrassed about Di?"

She looked down at the bulge that was still in my pants. She pointed at the wet spot, "I didn't think I would get that wet."

I refrained from laughing because that would only make her more embarrassed, "Don't be. I love that I have that effect on you. Trust me."

With my hands still on both sides of her face, I bent down and gave her a kiss on her forehead. "Now get inside before I take you home with me crazy girl."

"You're going to stop calling me crazy."

We both laughed as she went into her clutch purse to get her key. She took out her keys and unlocked the door.

Before opening it, she turned around and looked at me, "Call me when you get home ok Ace."

"I will Beauty, but I need to ask you something before you go inside."

She looked at me waiting for me to ask my question. "Did you mean what you said about you being mine?"

"Yes, I meant it. I'm yours Ace."

Pulling her back into me, I gave her a quick peck on the lips. That was all I could handle at the moment without losing self-control. "Thank you, Beauty."

We said our goodbyes and she disappeared behind the door. I waited until I heard her lock the front door from the inside to walk back to my car. After I got in my car, I sat there for a few minutes and thought about Ladi declaring that she was mine. Because I didn't want to ever lose her, I decided that I had to tell her about my relation to Saint sooner than later.

The minute I pulled into the parking garage of my condo at two fifteen in the morning, all I wanted to do was get in the shower and get in bed to call Ladi. It was too late to go back to Saint's place. He, Angel, and the twins were most likely sleeping. I had been staying there to avoid Sasha, but I needed to be back in my own space tonight. Before I got out of the car, I sent Ladi a text.

Me: Just made it home. I'm about to get in the shower. Let me know if you still want me to call you since you have to be up in a few hours.

She replied immediately.

Beauty: I just got out the shower so call me when you're done. I want to hear your voice before going to sleep.

Me: Will do Beauty. I want to hear yours too.

Putting my phone back in my pocket, I opened my door to get out. My phone vibrated as soon as it was in my pocket, but I decided to check it once I made it inside. I took the elevator to the twelfth floor. My condo was directly across from the elevator, and I was grateful for that tonight. My body was on a high from Ladi but also tired from the meetings I had with clients earlier that day.

As soon as I stepped out of the elevator my eyes immediately connected with Sasha's. It was past two in the morning, and she was standing outside of my door. The second she opened her mouth to start speaking, my blood began to boil.

"I see you finally decided to come home. Where have you been Ace? Hold up, is that lipstick on your lips? You're really sleeping with the help? Are you serious? After four years Ace? You are throwing four years away for your brother's help!"

I hadn't bothered removing the residue of Ladi's lip stain from my lips right away because I didn't need to. My plan was to go home and shower. It wasn't for Sasha to be outside of my door forcing me to engage in her drama. Yet, here she was.

Sasha asked question after question not giving me a chance to reply to one before asking another. I desperately wanted to just push her away from my door, but nothing was ever that simple with Sasha. Instead, I spoke to her as calmly as I could.

"Sasha I'm going to make this as clear as I can because I'm tired of dealing with you and your drama. You will not refer to Ladi as my brother's help ever again. She worked hard to be where she is. I'm not going to let you diminish that because you haven't accomplished anything in life. By no means am I trying to bring you down, but you will not discredit her success."

She opened her mouth to respond, but I cut her off before she could say a word. "You threw away the three years we were together by lying and cheating. You did, not me. This last year we were not together Sasha. Again, I apologize for taking the pieces of you that you offered to me from time to time. I shouldn't have done that to you because we both knew there would never be an us again. I accept my part but these crazy stunts you're pulling have to stop tonight Sasha. Chill your ass out."

"You love me Ace. I've been trying to convince you that we belong together. Is she really worth throwing our history away?"

If I hadn't known who Sasha was, I might've been more sympathetic. But, I did, therefore, I wasn't. "Sasha, leave her out of this! I've told you time and time again I didn't want this. You took from me what you could, and I did the same. How many times do we have to go over that?" I asked, feeling my frustrating building up.

"As many times as it takes for you to take me back," she answered.

"That is never going to happen! You knew that a year ago, six months ago, and it hasn't changed. Why would it?"

"I love you Ace!" She yelled.

"No, you love having control over me. You don't love me, you never did. I loved you Sasha, but that wasn't enough for you to be loyal."

Grabbing her arms, I moved her to the side. Luckily my keys were already in my hand. I quickly unlocked the door, and I went inside. Closing and locking the door behind me, I stripped out of my clothes and shoes right in the living room. Every thought I had of taking a shower went out the window. All I wanted to do was get in bed and call Ladi. If it were up to Sasha, I would be out there arguing with her all night. That was the kind of thing she lived for. Any attention she got from me fueled her craziness. I couldn't keep doing that with her anymore.

Once in my room, I took my phone out of my pant pocket, draped my clothes on the chest, and dialed Ladi's number. Ladi's voice would have to be enough to relax me since I was unable to be in her presence.

"Hello?"

Just as I thought, my body started to relax at the sound of her voice, "Beauty."

"You miss me already?" she asked. I heard her moving around, giving away that she was getting comfortable.

Laying down on my back I answered, "Whenever we're apart Di."

In four short days, Ladi gave me what I'd been needing for years. I'd never been the type of man to hold back my feelings or anything I had to say. Not necessarily impulsive but I always went for what I wanted. The fact that Ladi didn't resist me nor hide from me after the altercation with Sasha proved to me; she was worth all the effort I was making. I wanted her to always know the weight that held.

"Same here baby."

As soon as I heard her call me baby, I picked myself up by my elbows, "You know you can't ever call me Ace again." She started laughing, but I was serious.

"Stop playing." She said while still laughing.

"I'm dead ass, crazy girl."

"And you call me crazy?" She started laughing louder causing me to join her.

"You are crazy. I need to ask you something serious though Di."

She stopped laughing allowing me to continue, "Did you mean what you said Beauty? I need to be sure you meant what you said, and it wasn't because we were in the moment."

She took a deep a breath and exhaled before saying, "I

meant it, baby. Everything in me wants to see where this goes. Whether it's for the moment or forever, I'm yours."

"Which one would you prefer Di?"

Without hesitation, she replied, "Forever."

"Forever," I confirmed.

Boom Boom Boom

"Is that someone knocking at your door at two in the morning?" Ladi asked.

Before I could answer her, I heard Sasha's loud mouth, "Open the door Ace! I'm not going anywhere until you come talk to me!"

Thinking Sasha would just leave was my mistake. I was just hoping that someone would call security on her soon, so I wouldn't have to.

"Is that a female's voice?"

Feeling myself getting irritated, I pulled myself out of bed and sat at the edge, "Ladi, can I see you?"

"Baby..." she said.

I couldn't help but smile at the fact that she didn't call me by my name. "Facetime me, please."

As soon as I saw Ladi's Facetime call come through, I answered, "Do you trust me?"

I felt like a hypocrite asking her that because I was keeping something from her. But in order for me to explain to her what Sasha was doing outside of my door, she had to trust me.

I watched her eyes as I waited for her to answer, "Yes, I trust you baby. What's going on?"

I began explaining, "Since the argument with Sasha at Gayou's I haven't been staying at home. I knew she would show up at my condo because I blocked her from everything. It was the only way to avoid her. Tonight, I came home because I needed to be back in my own space. When

I got here, she was outside of my door. We exchanged a few words, but then I realized I was feeding into her drama. So, I moved her to the side and came in. I figured she would've just left."

After I was done with my explanation, I watched her to see how she would react. Ladi didn't say anything, so I opened my mouth to continue, but she spoke before I could.

"What are you going to do?" she finally asked.

"Nothing Di, I can't keep feeding into her. The only woman I'm going to invest any energy in is you Ladi."

She sighed and said, "I believe you, baby."

Those words meant the world to me, while simultaneously breaking my spirit. Here I was asking her to trust me, but I was keeping something from her. Tomorrow no matter what, I had to tell Di Saint was my older brother.

"Thank you, Beauty. I was hoping she would just leave. Someone will probably end up calling security on her soon though."

No sooner than I said that, I heard Sasha and the overnight security, Tim, yelling at each other. He was a heavyset older white man with red hair. Tim was one of those security guards that thought too highly of himself. Pride aside, I made a mental note to apologize to him whenever I saw him. Honestly, I was tired of having to continuously apologize for Sasha's actions. That was going to be the last apology I gave on her behalf.

Changing the subject, I said, "You look beautiful Di. I love that you're comfortable with me seeing you like this."

She had on an oversized T-shirt, and her hair was in a high ponytail with a black scarf wrapped around it. Every time I saw lady, I saw a new side of her physically. Every time I saw her, she showed me the many layers of Ladi. I was enjoying peeling her layers and discovering the parts of her that were untouched.

Before she could respond, there was a knock on my door. "That may be security; I'm going to check."

"Ok, do you want to call me back?" she asked.

I thought about it and said, "Nah, you're good Beauty. Stay with me."

Standing up, I went to my dresser and pulled out a pair of gray sweats. I quickly put them on and made my way to the door.

"I didn't think you owned any," Ladi said as I was walking down my hallway to the front door.

"Owned what?"

"Sweats. You're always dressed up."

Thinking back, I realized that every time Ladi and I saw each other I was dressed up. It was never intentional, but I always had some place to be that required me to. In four days, I had seen her in five different ways, yet she'd only seen me in two. In a way, that was who we were. I was established and who you saw was who you got. Ladi, on the other hand, was ever changing. She was discovering who she was, and I wanted to help create the path for her.

"Well, now you know crazy girl," I said to her as I opened my front door.

"Mr. Baptiste, I wanted to talk to you about your guest that I had to remove. Those types of guests are detrimental to the type of environment we are trying to uphold in our community." Tim said.

Trying not to get irritated, I rubbed my free hand down my face. Sasha wasn't my guest and for him to refer to her as that while Ladi was on the phone pissed me off.

"I apologize for the disturbance however, she wasn't my guest. I found her outside of my door when I got home earlier." I said through gritted teeth. The last thing I wanted was for Ladi to think that I had invited Sasha to my condo. The more he spoke, the more I started to regret that I hadn't agreed to have her call me back.

"Well Mr. Baptiste, according to your neighbors she's been coming here to wait outside your door the past few nights. This was the first time she's caused a disturbance, but we take these types of things seriously. I had to escort her out of the building. In addition, she's not allowed back in the building. The guest elevator code will be changed tonight so make sure to check your email for the new code."

"Got it."

Tim was trying to exercise his authority on me, but I wasn't going to give him the satisfaction of reacting. Sasha not being allowed in my condo was a blessing for the time being. Though it was only a temporary fix to my Sasha problem, it was only a matter of time before she popped up again. My house would be ready in about six months then I wouldn't have to worry about her at all. Six months felt like forever knowing how crazy Sasha could get.

"Be careful who you give the code to next time," Tim said.

With that, I shut the door in his face. Tim was blaming me for Sasha's actions just like everyone else, and that was not what I wanted to hear. It may have been rude to shut the door in his face, but that was better than the option of hemming him by his collar. I didn't tolerate disrespect well, Tim had a history of disrespecting some of my neighbors. He would do and say anything to prove his authority. At damn near three in the morning, I wasn't going to entertain him.

With the door closed, I leaned my back against it. Ladi

was looking at me with a blank expression. I went to say something, but she stopped me.

"Top flight security of the world looking ass!" she yelled and fell back in her bed laughing.

At first, I was surprised because I wasn't expecting that from her. But then I started laughing with her. This girl was everything. We both laughed for what seemed like minutes.

"What you know about checking crazy girl?" I asked once I was able to stop laughing.

"I know a little something. This girl that I was cool with in a class that I took my freshman year was from Tennessee. She checked people every chance she had. She acted like there was an art to it." Di said while laughing.

"There is an art to it. You did good though."

"I've been waiting for the perfect moment since you told me you were from Tennessee." Ladi was still laughing.

"You need to take your crazy self to sleep with all that laughing you're doing," I said.

"What? It was funny baby. You're right though. I'll text or call you tomorrow."

"Ok Beauty, you're mine, right? I asked.

"Forever." She responded.

"Forever Beauty."

I hung up the phone then made my way to my bed. Every conversation, every look, every interaction was confirmation that Ladi was the one for me.

❦ 11 ❦

Ladi

"I DIDN'T EXPECT YOU TO EXCEED MY EXPECTATIONS, but you did. That is why I am offering you the full-time position as Chez Saint's assistant general manager instead of the managerial position you applied for." Mr. Baptiste said.

Sitting across from him in his office, I tried to contain my excitement. When I woke up this morning to meet with Mr. Baptiste, I was not expecting him to offer me a better position. I rubbed my hands down the knee length dark gray pencil skirt I wore. Mr. Baptiste had informed me that I wouldn't start working today so instead of wearing all black, I chose to wear a dark gray skirt, a white loose fitting button-down short-sleeve blouse, and black sandal heels. Thankfully, it wasn't humid outside which meant my flat iron hair was still holding.

"Mr. Baptiste..."

He interrupted me, "Call me Saint. I don't really like people calling me Mr. Baptiste. That's my dad. I'd prefer to call you by your first name as well if you are comfortable with it."

"Yes, that's fine. You can call me Ladi."

He clasped his hands together on top of his desk, "Ladi it is. I'm not really with all that formal shit. Everybody here is relaxed with one another, and that's the atmosphere I want to keep. Keep it professional with the customers and relaxed with everyone else."

"Got it. Mr. Baptiste..."

He went to interrupt me, but I corrected myself, "I'm sorry. Saint, I'm just confused because I didn't know you were hiring an assistant general manager."

There was only one position available when I initially applied to Chez Saint, and the position he was giving me now wasn't it. The position that I applied for was the restaurant manager. Him offering this position meant I was assistant general manager of the restaurant and upstairs lounge.

"Initially, I wasn't. You made me change that Ladi. Like I told you before, you look great on paper. You're qualified for the position you applied for with your resume alone. I just had doubts when I saw you. However, when I saw how well you handled yourself during your trial run, I knew I needed you in a higher position."

I listened tentatively as he continued, "This position comes with a higher pay grade, a two-year contract that can be canceled within reason, and you'll be training the three managers that work under you. You are new here, but you have a lot to offer. You did some of what these managers would never think to do."

Nodding my head, I smiled, "Thank you again for the opportunity, Saint. You won't regret it."

"You're welcome again Ladi. The reason I asked you to come today instead of yesterday is so you could shadow my general manager, Chris. Mondays are his days off. He's waiting for you upstairs in the lounge. It's a short day for you so you can leave at two. Just make sure to see me so you can sign the contract before leaving."

"Yes, sir," I said as I stood up to leave his office and meet with Chris.

As I made my way upstairs to meet with Chris, thoughts of my night with Ace occupied my mind. Last night solidified all the feelings I had for Ace. Telling him that I was his wasn't something that I had planned. But every minute that I was around him, every time he touched me, every word he spoke to me, confirmed it for me. There wasn't a reason to hold anything back with him.

Ace had been in a relationship where he had invested everything and received nothing in return, and he was still giving love a chance. Never having experienced love from a man, I wanted the same untainted love that he did. The same pureness he saw in me, I saw in him. I couldn't deny that, nor did I ever want to. Forever meant forever to me.

The minute I entered the lounge, I pushed my thoughts of Ace to the back of my mind. Today I had to prove that I deserved the position as assistant general manager. This level of pressure to prove myself was one I'd never felt before. Saint basically promoted me before I signed my contract to work for him. Denying my ability to be the assistant general manager was something I would never do. I was just accustomed to people doubting me. Therefore I felt that I always had something to prove.

I made my way further into the lounge and noticed an

average height man who I assumed to be Chris standing at the bar. The lounge had the same silver and black color scheme as the restaurant. There were black leather booths that surrounded a small dance floor and stage. The two VIP sections were in the back, one on each side of the bar.

The man turned to face me as I got closer to him. His skin had a red tint to it. He had curly dark red hair and gray eyes. He wasn't unattractive, but his vibe seemed off.

"Ms. Thomas is it?" he asked.

"You can call me Ladi. You must be Chris?" I asked while stretching my hand out for a handshake.

He looked down at my hand and said, "In the flesh." Grabbing my hand, he shook it for a moment longer than I felt comfortable with.

I snickered nervously while removing my hand from his grasp. "Nice to meet you. Saint told me I would be shadowing you today."

A sly smirk appeared on his face, "You sure are sweetheart."

Not wanting to give him any indication that I was welcoming his flirting I said, "I prefer to be called either Ladi or Ms. Thomas."

Although I had never been in a committed relationship, it wasn't hard to recognize when a man was openly flirting with me. Shutting it down at the first sign of it was the best way to avoid it in the future. His grin fell immediately which meant he wasn't expecting that type of response from me. His already red face turned redder. His eyes showed signs of embarrassment and anger. His vibe that was already off turned into awkward silence between us.

Chris cleared his throat and said, "Follow me." His attitude was evident, but I always made it a point to remain professional in a professional setting. Chris spent the next four hours showing me what all my job would consist of. It was a lot of work, but I was sure in my abilities to handle the workload. My position would relieve some of his workload such as hiring new employees and making schedules. Whenever he was off, I would act as general manager.

Chris kept on emphasizing how he liked Chez Saint to be ran. The entire time he acted as if he was Saint himself. It was comical how he felt he had control over everyone and everything. Chris had to be the manager that didn't take others into consideration that Ashley had referred to.

Even though I was only supposed to shadow Chris, he sat down while I ran the restaurant during the lunch rush for two hours. Annoyed with his rude behavior, I was ready to get away from him as soon as possible. After the lunch rush, we were back in the lounge as he talked about what he expected from me as his assistant. Not the assistant general manager but his assistant.

Saint came walking in at 1:30 PM. "How did Ladi do?"

"She was cool. I just showed her around and showed her how you like things to be ran boss." Chris responded in a dry tone.

Chris had to be the biggest clown I had ever come across. He stood next to me and downplayed everything I did to Saint. Not only that, but not once had he mentioned to me how Saint liked things ran. I went to defend myself, but Saint spoke before I could.

"Nah, from what I heard she worked the hell out of the lunch rush. Better than it has been running in months." Saint looked at me and winked, but it wasn't a flirtatious wink. It was more as a sign to show he had my back.

I smiled, "I did what you asked me to do sir."

Looking back at Chris, I noticed he had a look of infuriation written all over his face. He quickly changed it as soon as Saint turned to face him as well. "Yeah, she was cool. I figured I'd give her a taste of what's to come." He said trying to explain himself.

"Just run it by me next time," Saint said.

His voiced dripped with sarcasm, "You got it, boss." Though Saint didn't appear to pick up on it, I did. Chris walked away and left me standing there with Saint.

Chris wasn't a good distance from us before Saint said, "Don't worry about that dry faced ass nigga."

Not sure if it was the shock from what he said, but I began laughing uncontrollably. Chris did have dry skin but the fact that I hadn't really noticed until Saint said it made me laugh harder.

"Don't get me wrong he works hard but I could tell he was in his feelings about something. This isn't the place for that. He knows how I like everything ran."

Finally, able to control my laughter, I nodded my head in agreement. Saint and I walked back down to his office for us to go over my contract. He informed me that as an assistant general manager my salary would be seventy thousand dollars a year before taxes. Because Chris had Sundays and Mondays off, I would work as the acting general manager in the mornings and afternoons on those days. Thursday and Friday nights were going to be my shifts as assistant general manager. Chris worked Tuesday, Wednesday, and Saturday nights. Therefore I was able to have them off.

Ashley was recently promoted to the restaurant manager. She and the lounge managers were able to handle their own shifts without much assistance. I would work four ten hour shifts weekly but depending how busy we were, I may end up working over the required forty hours. After I signed my contract, he welcomed me aboard, and I left for the day.

Whenever I made it home a little after three in the afternoon, my aunt was leaving for her shift at the hospital. She didn't give me a chance to tell her the great news about Saint offering me a better position before rushing off. Chasity only wanted to talk about her drama with Kenny which was understandable. She was moving back in three weeks, and I was ready to have my best friend close again.

Ace called me after I had texted him telling him I was headed home from the grocery store. He wanted full details on how my day went. Preferring to tell him details in person, we agreed that I would tell him everything over dinner. The excitement in his eyes every time I spoke about my passion was something I wanted to see in person. He and I decided that he would come over at five for an early dinner. I made him his favorite: oxtail and stew with white rice and fried plantains. His parents were from Saint Lucia which meant he would have high expectations for the oxtail.

It was thirty minutes before five, and I knew Ace would be arriving at any minute. Wanting tonight to be causal, I asked him not to dress up. He had explained to me that he was usually on the go dealing with clients most of the day and that was the reason that he dressed up a lot. It was always nice seeing a man dressed up, but I wanted to see him relaxed as well.

As I was fixing our plates, I heard the front door open. Figuring it was Ace since I told him I would leave the door unlocked for him, I yelled, "Baby, I'm in the kitchen! Go ahead and sit down; I'll be right there!"

I sat the plates down on the countertop and walked towards the living room. Ace was standing at the front door wearing a pair of black basketball shorts, a white v neck, and

Adidas slippers with matching white socks. His hair was still up in an updo. Although he was in more relaxed clothes, his stance still screamed power.

"Come here, crazy girl. You're trying to match my fly I see," he said while smiling.

I had on a pair of black high waisted leggings, a black and white sports bra, with long white socks. My thick hair was in a high bun at the top of my head. Smiling back at him I said, "I guess so. It wasn't intentional for sure."

Walking over to him, I went to hug him. He had his hands around his back, but when I wrapped my arms around his neck, he removed his right arm and wrapped it around my waist.

"I swear I couldn't wait to you see you Beauty, I've been thinking about you all day," he whispered in my ear,

My body weakened at his soft but commanding voice. "I've been thinking about you too baby."

I removed myself from his tight grip and said, "We're going to eat in the living room because tonight is going to be a chill night."

"That sounds perfect."

After I completely peeled myself from his hold, I had to catch myself from jumping up and down at the thought of having a relaxing night with him. Being around Ace made me feel warm on the inside. He made me want love more than I have ever wanted it before. Ace wasn't intimidated by the level of success I wanted to reach. Instead, he was finding ways to help me reach it. I admired that, I admired him.

He removed his left arm from around his back, revealing half a dozen red roses and half a dozen white roses mixed together. "These two colors given together represent unity. Last night, you told me that you're mine and I was yours the moment I laid eyes on you Beauty. I know you, and I aren't official yet, but we are forever Di."

He bent down and gently connected his lips with mine. It felt just as majestic as our first kiss. His lips were soft, but his kiss was aggressive and full of passion — the perfect contrast. Opening my mouth to let him in, I moved closer into him and wrapped my arms around his neck to hold him in place. Ace's tongue entered my mouth and satisfied every craving that I had. Our energy transferred to one another the deeper our kiss grew. The food that I had finished preparing was now a mere after-thought. Ace's touch was the only thing that was going to be able to feed the hunger that I was feeling in the pit of my stomach.

Ace's manhood grew harder as my love box got wetter. Just as quick as it started, he ended it. Breaking the kiss, Ace pulled away from me. Our eyes connected, and I saw myself falling in love with him in the future.

"Di, I don't want to rush you. It's taking all of my self-control not to have you bent over with your back arched right now."

I instantly started blushing, "It's taking all of my self-control not to be bent over for you right now."

Ace's eyes popped out of his head. I couldn't blame him because I shied away from talking about sex every time he made a reference to it. The truth was, it had been three years since I tried to have sex. My junior year at FIU was the one year that I actively dated, and it went terribly wrong. Kareem, a guy that I had dated for seven months, ruined my first sexual experience. He also ruined the three that followed. We'd begin, but as soon as he got the tip past the opening, I would stop him. He was too rough and didn't care about pleasing me. After trying four times, he gave up and stopped talking to me. I dated a few guys after him, but none of them got as far.

The boldness I was experiencing with Ace, I had no idea where it was coming from. He didn't know I was technically still a virgin, but I was ready to drop my panties as soon as our lips connected. There was a comfort that I felt with him that I had never experienced with any other man. Maybe that was why I was ready to give him every part of me. He knew what he wanted and wasn't shy about expressing it.

"Don't say things like that Di. I can't handle it." Ace leaned in and placed a soft kiss on my forehead.

Laughing at him, I took the flowers from him and said, "Just let me know when you can handle it then baby."

The biggest smile tugged at his lips, and he shook his head. It was evident that he was trying to take this side of me in. This side that even I was shocked by. With Ace, I didn't want to hold anything back. The way he drew me in with his words, smile, touch, I was ready and willing to give him everything he desired from me.

The most satisfying part was that it wasn't one-sided. Everything I wanted to do for this man, he wanted to do ten times more for me. My feelings for him did not go unreciprocated. He showed me in his touch, his consistency, and his persistence. He assured me with his words and his gestures that I wouldn't regret giving my all to him when I chose to.

Before Ace could respond, I went to the kitchen to fix our plates. I made sure to put extra oxtail on his plate. When I made it back to the living room, Ace was seated on the couch with the roses seated next to him. I sat both of our plates on the coffee table and picked up the roses.

"I'm going to go put these in water. What do you want to drink baby?"

"You got any Jack?" he asked.

"Yeah, I bought you some Jack. Luckily my aunt left as soon as I made it home. If she was here, I wouldn't have been able to put it in the fridge."

"You are one of a kind Ladi. Hurry up and put those up so we can eat crazy girl."

Ace had mentioned that his preferred drink of choice was Jack Daniel's whiskey and coke. According to him, it gave him the right type of buzz when he was sipping. If he was taking shots, he preferred shots of Crown. I normally didn't drink alcohol, but since tonight was a chill night, I fixed us both a drink.

"Are you serious? You couldn't wait on me?" I asked as soon as I returned to the living room. Trying not to yell, I took a deep breath.

"Di, I'm sorry. The oxtails were looking good, and you were taking too long." Ace said while stuffing his mouth with the food. He wasn't even using the fork I brought him.

I walked over and sat next to him. Looking down at my plate, I saw red. "You cannot be for real. Baby, I know you did not take some of my oxtails!"

Ace didn't bother to look at me. He kept eating and said, "You know oxtails are my favorite. No one told you to cook it so damn good crazy girl. We have to get you that restaurant ASAP."

"I should pour these drinks on you," I said with both cups still in my hand.

Finally looking up at me, he said, "You aren't that crazy."

Ace removed the cups from my hands and sat them on the coffee table. Inside, I was happy he was enjoying the food, but I was upset that even after giving him extra oxtails he still chose to eat from my plate.

"Please tell me you fixed me a plate to go home with." The enthusiasm in his voice resembled that of a child asking for a cookie.

"You're worrying about a to-go plate when you've eaten like ten pieces of oxtail already. There's still food on your plate!"

With a serious expression, he said, "They weren't big pieces."

My eyes grew big, "Baby those were big pieces! Stop lying!" causing us both to laugh hysterically.

"Ok, they were big Beauty. I just wasn't expecting them to be as good as they are."

We smiled at each other and continued to eat our food. As we sipped our drinks, I began to feel myself loosening up. Once we were done eating, Ace took our plates to the kitchen to clean them. I told him to leave them in the sink for me to wash later, but he refused, stating that cleaning up was the least he could do.

Upon returning to the living room, Ace picked me up from the couch, sat down, and proceeded to sit me on his lap. "Now, tell me about your day Beauty."

He had his arms draped around my waist while I laid my head on his chest. Taking in his natural scent, I said, "I got a position as the assistant general manager of the restaurant and lounge instead of as the restaurant manager I had originally applied for."

Ace pulled me away from his chest, allowing me to look up at him. He didn't look excited like I had expected. Unable to read his expression, I continued. "It's a better position with better pay. There are more responsibilities that come along with it, but I know I can handle them."

Ace sat there with a blank expression on his face. "What's wrong baby?" I asked.

For a few seconds, his mood seemed off, but he appeared to have gone back to his normal self immediately. As if he was snapping out of his own thoughts, Ace shook his head.

"Nothing Beauty." Still looking into my eyes, he continued, "I'm really happy for you. You deserve it, I know you do." At that moment I didn't regret waiting to tell him in person. His smile grew big, and his eyes lit up with excitement.

"Thank you, baby. The only bad part is having to deal with the general manager. I don't care for him at all. I was only supposed to shadow him today, yet he had me managing during the lunch rush. I didn't mind, but he later tried to make it seem as if I spent the whole day watching him. Thankfully, the owner had already heard about what happened during the lunch rush."

"That's messed up. Is that all he did Di? You seem like you're holding something back."

Trusting in Ace, I decided to tell him the other reasons I didn't care for Chris. "I don't trust him. One, he kept telling me how he liked things ran instead of how Saint liked things ran. Then, he kept calling me his assistant. But the icing on the cake was when he tried to flirt with me. After I immediately shut that down, he felt the need to be insolent towards me the rest of the day because of it."

Ace's eyes turned black, and his breathing became heavy, he mumbled something under his breath.

"Baby, I'm good. I promise." I assured him.

With both of my hands, one on each cheek, I pulled him down to my lips. I straddled his lap, immediately feeling the swelling in his basketball shorts harden. His body began to get rid of the built-up tension just like I wanted it to. Opening my mouth, I invited him to take control. With our tongues intertwined, Ace flipped me on my back and deepened our kiss.

He only removed his lips to say, "Ladi, I'm not going to rush you. I just want to taste you tonight. That's it, no matter how much further I want to go. Can I do that?"

I didn't have the courage to speak, so I nodded my head to grant him permission. He returned his lips to mine as his hands traveled down my body. He used his right hand to caress my left breast. Occasionally pinching my nipple bringing me both pleasure and pain. He slowly removed his lips from mine and placed them on my neck. His wet tongue against my skin put me in a state of bliss. As his hands roamed further down my body so did his lips. Once he made it to my waist, he looked up at me.

"You are mine right Beauty? I need you to say it."

"I'm yours, baby."

"Forever?" he asked.

"Forever."

Ace began to take off my leggings and panties simultaneously. My body instantly shuddered at his touch as his hands grazed my thighs. They were rough but also had a gentleness to them. The lower he went, the more my body melted to his touch.

As soon as they were both off, he threw them on the floor. Spreading my legs apart, Ace stared at me with the most intense gaze. It was evident he was holding back, but I understood why. This wasn't a simple sexual act, it was a true act of intimacy. The connection that our souls felt was going to turn physical. We would no longer be able to have any doubts about what we felt for each other. This was me giving him a very important part of me, and him fully accepting it. The hesitation was apparent in his eyes because after what he was about to do, losing ourselves to one another was inevitable. With one last glance, he assured me he was going to handle my body with care.

As his head moved closer to my bare mound, the harder it was for me to breathe. The moment the tip of his tongue slipped in between my folds, I completely stopped breathing. The motion of his tongue left me paralyzed. I was under his control, and he knew it. He spread my legs further apart and buried his face deeper. Unable to speak, unable to move, I laid there with tears rolling down my face as I enjoyed the sensation that Ace was giving my body. My body was no longer mine, it was his.

Ace slowly began to suck and a moan that I had been dying to release finally escaped from me. I could feel my climax building as the sensation in between my legs intensified. My eyes closed as I allowed my orgasm to take over me. My back arched, and my body began to convulse as I released my nectar into Ace's mouth which he accepted hungrily.

Allowing my body time to come down from my Ace induced high, I laid there with my eyes closed as he cleaned me with his tongue. Once he was done, I felt him stand up. As quickly as I felt his absence, I felt his presence again. When I was able to fully open my eyes, Ace was squatting in front of me with a wet washcloth. He laid soft kisses on my inner thighs as he used the washcloth to finish cleaning me.

"Let's go to my room."

Ace stopped wiping me and looked up, "Beauty, as badly as I want to do that, I can't. We both know you aren't ready. There's no reason to rush it. Forever right?"

"Forever," I responded while nodding my head.

He nodded in agreement and smiled at me. Ace sat the

washcloth on the floor, picking up my panties. "Stand up for me Di."

With the little energy I had left, I stood up in front of Ace. He lifted my right leg and began to put my panties on for me. I started to help him, but he stopped me. "I got this."

As his hands journeyed up my legs, chills traveled down my spine. Ace's touch was tender but powerful. His eyes moved at a much slower pace up my body than his hands. The appreciation in them made me smile. The only assistance that I offered to him was lifting my legs up as he put my panties back on for me. He did the same thing with my leggings.

After I was fully dressed, Ace picked up the washcloth that he had sat on the floor and left down the hallway towards the back of the house. When he returned, he sat down next to me and drew me close to his body. My body against his alleviated me in a way that nothing else could.

"What time is your aunt getting off work Di?" Ace asked.

"Six in the morning. She's working a double tonight."

"Wow, does she normally work like that? What does she do?"

"Auntie Marie is a housekeeper. She's never said it, but I know the reason she works as much as she does is because of me. It's always been the two of us, but now it's my turn to take care of her." I said answering his question.

"That's beautiful Di; you'll be able to do that for her soon." Ace leaned down and kissed my forehead.

We spent the rest of the night talking and getting to know each other more. The more we talked, the more connected I felt to him. He went more in detail about his past relationships including the one with Sasha. It was hard to believe that he wasn't more guarded with his heart due to all of the dishonesty in that relationship. Ace explained to me that he didn't allow that experience to turn his heart cold because his heart was never hers to have. It made sense because a person shouldn't have control over a heart that didn't belong to him or her. They would be able to misuse it but never truly destroy it. Only the owner would have that power but would never use it. Ace admitted that he knew his heart was mine, but time was the only thing that could determine when I would have it completely.

Before I knew it, hours had passed, and I had fallen asleep next to Ace on the couch. The only reason I woke up was because I felt Ace's large arms picking me up bridal style.

"I don't remember falling asleep," I said in a groggy voice.

"We both fell asleep. I'm going to put you in bed and then head out."

"What time is it?" I asked as I laid my head against his chest.

"It's two in the morning. Which room is yours?"

"The first one on your right baby."

Ace walked down the hallway with me in his arms, and I allowed myself to sink in further in his arms. He held me firmly as he opened the door to my bedroom. Once we were inside, he gently laid me on my bed and began looking around my room. I scooted to the middle of the bed as I watched him walk around my room.

"Your room looks like you're still in college Beauty," he said before chuckling.

"Well, I did move back only a month ago today. What did you think it was going to look like?"

"I don't know honestly. This room says a lot about you. I

love discovering new things about you, and I'm able to see a lot of the layers that you are made of through it."

Ace walked to the left side of my room where he noticed a photo box with his name sitting on top of my cherry wood chest. He walked back over to the center of my bedroom and sat at the end of my bed. I crawled down to join him.

"I can explain," I said before he could ask me any questions about the box. "That's where I keep the greeting cards you've given me. That box that it was next to is where I keep the greeting cards I've collected over the years, but I wanted to put yours in their own box. It's lame, I know." I went to get the box from him, but he pulled it away.

Ace bent down and planted a soft kiss on my forehead. It was a warm gesture that he began to do often. Always gentle. Always when it was needed. Always a reassurance of his feelings for me.

"Not lame, sweet. I get why you do it Ladi. Don't be embarrassed. Can I ask you why you started to collect greeting cards?"

I knew that question was going to come eventually, I just wasn't sure how to answer it. No one ever asked because no one knew that I collected greeting cards. Instead of answering him, I got up from the bed and went to retrieve the other box. Opening it, I took out the greeting card that was on top. I walked back over together with me sitting to the right of him. Since he was centered in the middle, Ace was taking up most of my full-size bed. Handing him the card, I watched as he opened and read it. When he was done, he looked at me with sadness in his eyes.

"That is the last greeting card my mom gave me on my second birthday. The greeting cards she gave me my first two years of life are my daily reminders of how much she and my dad loved me. Collecting greeting cards didn't start until I was five. I was finally able to read, and my appreciation for words came along with it. The words in that card mean everything to me." Out of my control, tears began to form in my eyes.

I quickly wiped away the tears as soon as they began to run down my cheeks. Each tear that I wiped away, another one followed instantly. My emotions were all over the place as I began to sob silently. Ace wrapped his arms around me while kissing my tears away. His kisses comforting me and his touch healing the pain that I had never spoken of.

"I'm sorry Di. I wouldn't have asked..."

I cut him off before he could respond, "No, thank you. I have been holding on to that for years."

"What are you thanking me for exactly Beauty? I'm the reason you're crying."

"Thank you for helping me release this pain, for opening me up to a chance at love, for appreciating the different sides of me, kissing my tears away. Everything."

We sat there in silence as Ace hugged me tighter. He held on to me as if he could squeeze out all the pain I felt inside. "Forever Beauty."

That was all I needed to hear. As soon as forever fell from his lips and onto my ears, I knew exactly what I needed. "Can you spend the night with me?"

"Are you sure? I don't want to disrespect your aunt's house."

Turning my neck sideways I asked, "You're kidding right? Do you not remember what took place in the living room a few hours ago?"

We both started laughing causing him to finally let me go, "I remember crazy girl. Her coming home to me walking out of your bedroom is different Beauty."

"True but you can just leave at six before she gets home from work."

The reluctance was written on his face, but he said, "I can do that. There are a few meetings I have scheduled in the morning anyway."

Asking Ace to spend the night with me was a bold move. It would take a lot of self-control on both of our parts for nothing to happen. I just wanted him next to me because I didn't want to start thinking about the loss of my parents anymore. Whoever said, you couldn't miss something you never had was wrong. Being around Ace, made me realize that more and more. He opened me up to emotions I didn't even know I possessed. Feelings I never knew I had. Yearning for a love I didn't know existed.

Standing up, I walked over to the chest and put the card back in the box. I removed an oversized t-shirt from one of the drawers and put it over my sports bra. Once it was completely on, I removed my sports bra from underneath and leggings. When I turned back around, Ace was staring at me.

"What?" I asked.

He pointed to the center of my hips, "You know I just had my lips on her right?"

I stared at him as he continued pointing at my chest, "But you are over there hiding them from my eyes. You should've seen how crazy you looked taking off your sports bra with your shirt on." He shook his head and chuckled.

Ignoring him, I walked over to the right side of my bed and slipped under the comforter. Ace stood up, pulled his phone out of his pocket and sat it on the nightstand. He then took his shirt off and got in the bed next to me. He laid down to the left of me on his back with a look of discomfort plastered on his face.

"Why are you looking like that?" I asked him.

"Ladi, I'm 6'3 and two hundred and thirty pounds sharing a full-size bed."

He was serious, but I couldn't help but laugh at how uncomfortable he looked. "I didn't think about that."

"We're getting you at least a queen. You're too old to have a full-size bed Di. My feet are hanging off the bed. You're lucky you're so little or else you wouldn't have any room to sleep."

I held myself up by my elbows to see that his feet were hanging off the end of bed. "You're right, I do need a bigger bed. I'm going to get one soon, I promise baby."

After kissing him on his cheek, I turned my back towards him. I felt him turn himself towards me and used his arm to pull me in close to his body. It was firm and hard. My body shivered as he pulled me tighter into his. As usual, my body began to warm up as it relaxed under his touch. His manhood began to harden causing me to pull away from him to create space between us. He knew I wasn't ready, but I had to tell him why I wasn't ready.

"There's something I have to tell you baby," I said without turning around to face him.

"Tell me." His voice was low, and I could tell he was getting sleepy.

Sighing heavily, I said. "Technically I'm still a virgin."

"Technically?" he asked with curiosity in his voice.

"I tried having sex three years ago. Before I could actually lose it, I stopped it. All four times." Not sure how Ace would respond, I remained quiet waiting to see if he would say anything before I continued.

"I knew that you were a virgin. Well, I suspected that from the way you reacted every time I brought up sex, you feel me. That's why I'm not trying to get inside of you right now. You need to be ready to give yourself to me. Just know that you weren't his to have Beauty, you were always mine. When I feel that you're ready, you won't even have to tell me. I'll know, and there won't be any stopping. Trust me."

He pulled me back into him, and I let him. Ace said all there was to say. I let his words replay over and over in my head as I drifted off to sleep in his arms.

❦ 12 ❦

Ladi

ACE'S CELLPHONE THAT WAS ON MY NIGHTSTAND WOKE us up out of our sleep. Removing his arm from around me, Ace hauled himself up to answer the phone.

"Fuck." Ace mumbled under his breath. "Hello?" he answered his phone before I could ask him what was wrong.

I couldn't hear what the person was saying but could feel Ace's body tensing up next to me. I rolled over so that I could read his facial expressions. "Get off my line with that bullshit." was all that he said before hanging up the phone.

Ace looked at me and answered my questions before I could ask. "Sorry about that. I'm

frustrated. It's seven, and I have a meeting at eight. That's on me though, I didn't think to set my alarm."

"Shit, my aunt should be home by now," I said.

"That's my second time hearing you curse." Ace said while laughing. I rolled my eyes at

him and quickly got myself out of bed.

Getting out of bed, I went down the hall to my aunt's room and knocked on the door. No answer. After waiting a few more seconds, I opened her bedroom door only to find that the room was empty.

"Beauty." I turned around to find Ace standing in the hallway. "Her car isn't outside.

Maybe she's working later than you thought."

"Yeah, you might be right baby. Works out though since we overslept." I said while walking towards him. "Who was that on the phone anyway?"

Ace looked down at me as I wrapped my arms around his waist. He let out a breath of frustration, "Sasha called me from a different number since I blocked hers. She was talking crazy, but I'm not entertaining it."

That was the only flaw that I saw in Ace, Sasha. She brought unnecessary drama that I refused to deal with. Ace kept reassuring me that he had her under control, but that was evidently wrong. "Baby, you keep saying that, but it doesn't seem like it. My feelings for you are getting stronger, but I can't deal with petty drama."

"Relax Beauty. I told you I had it handled. It's handled." He wrapped his arm around my neck and kissed the top of my head.

"I'm relaxed. It's just a reminder."

"Noted. But I'm going to go ahead and head out. Thank you for asking me to spend the night. Regardless of sleeping in that small ass bed, that was the best sleep I've ever gotten. How do you expect me to sleep without you in my arms every night after last night?" he asked with a sneaky grin.

"The same way you slept every night before me."

"There's no going back for me Beauty. Forever." "Forever." I agreed.

Ace and I walked hand in hand to the front door. He promised to call me once he was done with his meetings. We gave each other a quick peck on the lips before Ace left out to head to his car. Locking the door behind me, I made my way back to bed. I was beyond thankful that I was off today because I was going to go right back to sleep.

I ROLLED OVER IN MY BED FEELING ANNOYED AS MY phone vibrated on the nightstand. It was as if waking up to a vibrating phone was the only way to wake up today. My plan was to get as much rest as possible before seeing Ace for lunch at his office. He had called me after his meeting with his client at nine to ask me if I could meet him for lunch at one o'clock. It was now eleven in the morning, and all I wanted was one more hour of sleep.

Grabbing my phone from the nightstand, I noticed that it was Jackson Memorial Hospital calling. My aunt had only called me from her work phone a few times in the past.

"Hello?" I quickly answered.

"May I speak to Ladi Thomas." the woman on the phone asked.

"This is she."

"Good morning Ms. Thomas. My name is Dr. Kelly McDarment. I was calling regarding your aunt, Marie Thomas."

My heart sunk to the bottom of my feet. No one at the hospital ever called about my aunt. An uneasy feeling swept over my body, and I started to feel nauseous. "Is my aunt ok? Can I speak to her?"

"Unfortunately, I can't go into details over the phone. What I can say is, she has been admitted into the hospital. You were listed as her emergency contact, so it would be best if you come as soon as possible Ms. Thomas."

It felt like someone had punched me in my chest and took all the air out of my body. I couldn't form any words to respond to the doctor as tears started to fall down my face. My aunt, the one person that I knew would always be in my corner, was laying in a hospital bed. Trying to process what she had just told me about my aunt felt surreal.

"Ms. Thomas are you still there?" Dr. McDarment asked breaking me out of my thoughts.

"Uhm." I cleared my throat, "I'm on my way."

Before she could respond, I hung up the phone. I rushed to the dresser to grab a pair of leggings and ran to the bathroom to brush my teeth. After getting dressed in record time, I grabbed my purse along with my keys that were hanging by the front door and ran out of the house. I sped all the way to the hospital, but it felt like it took an eternity to get there. As soon as I parked, I ran through the double doors straight to the information desk. There was an older white woman with long blond hair sitting and talking to an older black woman with a short afro.

"Hi, my name is Ladi Thomas. Can I get the room number for Marie Thomas please?" "Yes, you can. You must be Ms. Marie's niece. You look just like her." The older white
woman said.

Not wanting to come off as ill-mannered, I responded, "Yes ma'am."

I waited impatiently as she looked up the room that my aunt was in. When she finally told me that her room number was six hundred and three, I ran towards the elevator. Mentally preparing myself for the worst but hoping for the best, I took a deep breath as I waited for the it. Once in the elevator, I pushed the button to take me to the sixth floor. The entire time I was silently praying that all would be ok with my aunt. I needed her here with me. There were things that I needed to do to pay her back for all the sacrifices she made for me.

The elevator doors finally opened, and I ran down the hallway. As soon as I made it to room six hundred and three, a female doctor was coming out of it. She was tall and slender with long curly black hair that made her pale skin look ghostly. Her face was long and oval.

"Is this Marie Thomas' room?" I asked as I peered over her shoulder trying to see into the

room.

"You must be Ladi Thomas. I'm Dr. McDarment; we spoke over the phone." She

extended her hand for me to shake and I did. Simply nodding my head, I remained quiet in hopes that she would tell me about my aunt.

"Ms. Marie is getting some much-needed rest, but there are a few things that I wanted to discuss with you. Marie had a seizure this morning. Do you know if she is prone to having seizures?"

Hurriedly shaking my head, I answered, "No, my aunt has never had a seizure before."

"Well Ms. Thomas, Marie had a seizure this morning right before leaving from her shift. One of our nurses found her. An MRI scan was conducted to see if there were any abnormalities that may have caused the seizure. We did find a mass on her frontal lobe. Now, we aren't sure whether it's cancerous or not, but tests are being run. We'll be able to give you more information once the results come in." she said in a sad tone with sympathy in her eyes.

That was a lot for me to process. My aunt had a seizure, and a mass was found on her brain. I was sleeping peacefully in Ace's arm while my aunt was all alone after having a seizure. A mixture of sadness and rage washed over my body, and I fell to the floor weeping uncontrollably.

At that moment, my whole world came crashing down. My aunt was my world. She was the reason I was who I was. Auntie Marie pushed me to be better, encouraged me, and she gave me the only love I knew. Now I stood a chance of losing all of that.

The doctor kneeled next to me, "Ms. Thomas I know this is a lot to take in, but you have to be strong for your aunt. I have worked with her for years, and she is a positive person. We don't know how bad this is yet, until we have definite answers, remain positive." She patted my back twice, stood up, and walked away.

Trying to get myself together before standing up to walk into the room, I took three deep breaths. The doctor was right, I needed to be the strength my aunt had always been for me. The mass could be cancer, but then again it could be benign. Until I knew for sure which one, I was going to only think positively.

I opened the door to Auntie Marie's room. She looked peaceful laying down in the hospital bed. I grabbed one of the chairs next to the window and sat it next to her bed. As soon as I sat down, I reached for her right hand placing it into both of mine. Guilt began to consume me because I wasn't there for her when she needed me the most. Granted, I didn't know that she was going to have a seizure, but it still bothered me that I was with Ace instead of her.

"Stop thinking so hard cherie." Auntie Marie said in a low voice. Both of her eyes were still closed

"Auntie, I am so sorry."

"Ladi what are you sorry for?" "Not being here."

She slowly opened her eyes, "Cherie there is nothing for you to be sorry for. I know as soon as they called you, you came. Yesterday was your first day at your job. You should have been celebrating with that tall man."

Forcing a light giggle, I said, "His name is Ace."

"Were you with Ace?" she asked. I nodded my head, and she continued, "Good. That's exactly where you should've been. I love you cherie. I gave you everything that I could, but there are things that I couldn't. You need to embrace love from other people. I didn't do that, and I don't want that for you. Working hard is important but you need true love, a family, you need more than just me. You gave all that to me cherie, but I can't be the only one to give that to you. Ace can, and he will. It's in his eyes when he looks at you."

That was the first time my aunt expressed why she began putting pressure on me to be more open to dating. To my knowledge, my aunt had never been married nor had any children, I was her sole focus. Sure she dated, but I never met any of the men. Auntie Marie worked all the time to take care of me but never took the time to care for herself.

"You are my greatest gift Ladi. I've never told you certain things, but I am going to tell you them now because life is too short. When I was twenty, I was in love and got married to a man I thought was the love my life. I was proven wrong after having a miscarriage. Being told I wasn't going to able to get pregnant again after the miscarriage broke me."

She paused for a few seconds and continued, "My ex-husband didn't hide his hatred for me after that. He treated me poorly and eventually I had to make the decision to leave him. I thought love would never come for me again. Every chance I took failed, but then when I was twenty-five, you gave me the love I had been missing Ladi. I lost my younger sister, but I had you. I'm telling you all this to say, don't feel guilty for being with him while I was here. I found my missing love the day you came to live with me. You just found yours. Never feel guilty for discovering it because I will never feel guilty for getting the chance to raise you."

Love wouldn't be how I described what I felt for Ace, but I wasn't going to argue with my aunt about it. She had just told me things about her life that I never knew. We were the only immediate family we had. I appreciated her even more than I ever had after revealing this new information. My aunt always knew exactly what I needed to hear to get me back in a good head space. Before I could respond the door to her room opened. A light skin shapely nurse with a short pixie cut came through the door.

"How are we feeling Ms. Marie?" she asked my aunt.

"Tired but I'm making it. Ladi, this is the nurse that found me." My aunt pointed in her direction, and we made eye contact.

"Ladi? Did you go to FIU?" the nurse asked.

With confusion written on both of our faces, I answered, "I did."

"It's me, Angel! We had Professor Philips' management course together!" She
exclaimed.

"This is a small world." my aunt said covering her mouth in disbelief. "Wow. I didn't recognize you with the short hair." I said addressing Angel.

"I cut it after having my twins two years ago. You look different too but with a name like

Ladi, nobody can forget meeting you." she stated while smiling.

Angel and I had a management class during my freshman year at FIU. She took the class as a GPA booster because her major didn't have anything to do with management, hence her being a nurse now. She and I used to converse while we were in class but never outside of it. We weren't friends, but we were definitely close associates.

"Congratulations. Also, thank you for finding my aunt." I said squeezing my aunt's hand

as she laid there watching Angel, and I converse.

"You don't have to thank me. I'm glad I found her when I did. Ms. Marie is the sweetest person I know. We all love working with her although I think she works way too hard." She walked closer and put her hand on my aunt's left shoulder.

"I tell her that all the time."

Auntie Marie looked from me to Angel and with a low voice said, "And I have told you

both, there is no such thing as working too hard."

Both Angel and I shook our heads at my aunt. She drifted off to sleep soon after leaving Angel and I the chance to really catch up. Mostly reminiscing on college, we didn't go into details about our personal lives. We exchanged contact information and agreed to have lunch in the near future. She left giving me a chance to call Ace while my aunt was still sleeping. I stepped outside and dialed his number.

"Beauty," he answered.

"Baby." unintentionally, my voice began to crack.

"Talk to me, mama."

Sighing heavily I said, "We're going to have to reschedule lunch. My aunt had a seizure.

I'm with her at the hospital now."

"Which hospital Beauty? Is she ok? I'll cancel all my meetings for the day and come to

you."

Although I appreciated Ace's willingness to drop everything for me, I wanted this alone

time with my aunt. I was still feeling guilty for being with Ace and not with her. "I kind of want

some alone time with my aunt."

After a few seconds of silence, he said, "I understand."

Not wanting to offend him, I explained, "Don't take it the wrong way. I just want to make sure she's ok and spend some alone time with her."

"I understand Beauty. Let me know if you need me. Please keep me updated."

"I will. I'll text you later." We said our goodbyes and I hung up the phone before returning to my aunt's room. Auntie Marie was laying there with her eyes still closed. I returned to my seat and watched her sleep for what seemed like hours. Ace had called and texted, but I ignored all of them. The guilt that I was feeling wasn't because of him, but then again it was. Not only that, my aunt was the only person that I had to comfort me during tough times. Ace was trying, but I didn't know how to let him in.

My phone started vibrating for the fifth time, and it was Ace calling again. I ignored his call and turned my phone off. "Turn the phone back on Ladi." my aunt said in a bleary voice startling me.

"Auntie!"

She cleared her throat, "Ladi turn the phone back on and let that man know I'm ok. You will not push him away because you feel guilty about something that you didn't have any control over."

"Auntie I can't."

"Ladi, let this be the only time I tell you this. No matter where you were or who you were with, the seizure was inevitable. Don't allow your irrational guilt to cause you to lose something special. Would you have quit your job if it happened while you were at work?" I shook my head no. "Exactly. Now turn on the phone, step outside, and call him back."

Listening to my aunt, I stood up and stepped outside of her hospital room to return Ace's call. My guilt may have been unreasonable, but it was there, nonetheless. Conveying that to Ace seemed like it would be hard to do. My intentions weren't to push him away, but my actions proved otherwise.

Once outside of the room, I turned my phone back on. It was now a little after six in the evening. Before dialing Ace's number, I mentally prepared everything I wanted to say to him. When I felt that I had gotten my thoughts together, I dialed his number. He answered immediately, "Beauty."

He didn't sound mad; the only emotion that I heard in his voice was sadness. "I'm sorry

I've been ignoring you all day. I can explain." I quickly said.

"There's nothing to explain. You're feeling guilty because we were together this

morning. Your way of dealing with that is by pushing me away, and I get that Di. What I need you to

get is that it's not that easy to push me away. I wanted you since I laid my eyes on you and now that I have you, I'm not letting you go. If you need space, I will give that to you. But we're

forever, remember?"

As if he could see me through the phone, I nodded my head. "Can I see you?"

Within seconds Ace was calling me on Facetime. Quickly answering the phone, I slid down the wall and sat on the floor with my legs pulled up to my chest. "How you are feeling crazy girl?"

"Truthfully?"

"I always want the truth from you Di," he answered.

"I'm scared baby. They found a mass on her frontal lobe which was the cause of the seizure. We're waiting to find out if it's malignant or benign, but either way, she has to have surgery to get it removed." I closed my eyes to keep the tears from escaping.

"I can't imagine what you're going through Ladi. Open your eyes, I need you to look at

me when I say this next thing."

Opening my eyes, I examined Ace's face that held a serious expression, "Whatever you need, I will take care of it. Whether it's wiping your tears away or to be your strength, I'm not going anywhere Di. It's ok to be scared because you were faced with the possibility of losing your aunt. Try to remain positive and if you can't, know that I am willing to bring positivity to

you."

I had been ignoring him all day yet here he was willing to be the strength that I desperately needed. Ace was actively trying to be present for me in my time of need. I needed him more than I even realized I did. Each word penetrating my soul and planted seeds of hope. "Thank you for that baby. I needed to hear that more than you know."

"You're welcome Beauty. I'm going to give you your space, but I really needed to check on you. Go back in there with your aunt and keep me updated if you can. Just remember I'm here for you Di."

"Forever." "Forever," he stated.

I hung up the phone and took a few moments to myself before going back in. Ace's words stuck with me. It felt good knowing that I had him in my corner. He didn't make me feel bad for ignoring him. Instead, he understood why I did it without me having to explain. Looking back, it was irrational of me, but hindsight is always 20/20.

After five minutes, I stood up and went back to my aunt's room. She was back sleeping peacefully as I waited for the doctor to come talk to me about the results of her test.

❧ 13 ❧

ce

THREE WEEKS HAD PASSED SINCE LADI'S AUNT HAD
been hospitalized. The first week after everything happened
was hard. In the beginning, Ladi wanted to shut me out.
When she did try to let me be there for her, I could tell she
didn't know how. The second week went more smoothly
which gave us the opportunity to become closer. She
opened herself to me in ways that I didn't think were possible. Ladi gave me the chance to know all her fears, weak-
nesses, and vices; making herself completely vulnerable to
me. By week three, I was falling for Ladi harder than I
expected to. She was my obsession, and I couldn't go a day
without talking to her or seeing her face.

While her aunt was in the hospital, we Facetimed at
least four times a day. Ladi didn't allow me to come to the

hospital. Whenever I asked to visit, she would tell me she wanted her focus to solely be on her aunt. She wouldn't even tell me the name of the hospital to avoid me trying to go there. With good reason, because I would've shown up. Her guilt was the reason she felt that way, and I couldn't fault her for it. Respecting her wish for space was extremely difficult because it wasn't something I wanted. However, I did my best to give it to her while making myself available whenever she needed my support.

Every evening after leaving the hospital she would meet me at her aunt's house. We would spend the night together talking until sleep took over us. On the nights she had to work, I would meet her at her home to spend the night as well. I ended up buying Ladi a king size bed and had it delivered to her house after having to spend two nights on the full-size mattress. I was way too big to try and share a full-size bed with Ladi every night.

Di's aunt was released from the hospital three days ago. The mass the doctors had found was benign. The surgery to remove the noncancerous mass was successful, and she was expected to make a full recovery. The only negative, I was back to sleeping alone. It didn't feel right not having her under me as I slept. Ladi would literally squeeze her body under mine. Having her small frame under me was the only way I could sleep comfortably. It wasn't until our first night apart did I realize just how much I wanted that. I was already planning on a way to get Ladi to spend the night at my place since she had a twenty-four hour on-call nurse for her aunt.

To make things better, Sasha had completely fallen off the grid. Not having to worry about Sasha's drama permitted Ladi and me to enjoy the foundation that we were building for when we decided to make things official. We agreed to continue to learn each other without titles. The way I saw it, there wasn't a reason to rush us. Title or not Ladi was mine, and I was hers. It was only a matter of time before I made it official. It was coming soon. Very soon.

She was doing a great job of balancing her time between her aunt, me, and her new job. Because Di had just started at Chez Saint, she chose not to take time off from work. Saint would've given her a couple of days off, but she never asked. She never even mentioned to Saint anything about her aunt's ailment. Whenever I had spoken to him about it, he wanted to give her a few days off but couldn't. I had yet to tell Ladi that Saint was my older brother which meant he wouldn't be able to explain how he found out about her aunt.

My plan was to tell her during our lunch date three weeks ago, but it was canceled due to her aunt being hospitalized that same day. With the stress of her aunt being in the hospital, her having surgery, and starting a new job, the timing to tell her was never right. My conscience was eating at me more and more as the days passed because Ladi was transparent with me about everything. I was opening myself to her as well, but that was the one thing I couldn't find a way

to tell her.

"I'm so excited," Ladi said while clutching her hands together, breaking me out of my thoughts. I looked over at her sitting in the passenger seat of my black Infiniti QX70. Her hair was back in a wild mane which I grew to love more than anything. She was wearing a pair of black leggings and a green Michigan State University shirt. As usual, I was dressed up being that I had a couple of meetings later in the day. My dreads were hanging loose. I wore a pair of tailored black slacks, a navy-blue button down, and black oxfords.

We were on our way to Miami International Airport at nine in the morning to pick up her best friend who was moving back to Miami. Ladi had asked me to drive because my second car, an SUV, was bigger than her Camry. She was afraid she wouldn't have enough space in her car for her friend's luggage.

"Really? I couldn't tell." I said while giving her a small smile. For the past week, her best friend moving back to Miami was all Di talked about. I was happy her friend was coming into town. I just wasn't happy that I would have to share my time with her.

She playfully shoved my right arm, "Ha-ha, very funny."

"You know I'm just messing with you Beauty." Ladi was my breath of fresh air. She didn't allow my feelings for her to go in vain. Di appreciated the affection, the small gifts, my time, and every effort I made to keep a smile on her face. We never had the chance to fight our feelings for one another. Once we realized we were both in, we embraced them fully.

"Yeah, I know. Thank you for rearranging your schedule to come with me to pick up Chas."

Giving her a questioning look I stated, "You didn't give me much of an option crazy girl. You refused to drive my car after I offered it to you."

"I didn't want to drive it, baby. What's wrong with that?"

"The reason you didn't want to drive it is the problem," I answered.

"What if something happened to your car while I was driving it?" she asked with genuine worry.

Not bothering to look over at her I responded, "I'm trusting you with my heart Di. Why

wouldn't I trust you with my car?" I felt her small hand reach for my mine. Lifting it, I brought her hand up to lips to plant a soft kiss. I squeezed her hand before laying it down on my thigh as we immersed ourselves in the silence that was created by my declaration.

Pulling up in front of the arriving flights I recognized a familiar face but couldn't exactly place where I had met the person. As soon as I parked, Ladi jumped out and ran directly to the person I was sure I knew from somewhere. I unbuckled my seatbelt before getting out of the car to help who I assumed was her best friend with her bags. When I made it up to them, they were pulling apart from each other. Ladi spun around grabbing my hand and dragged me closer to her, "Chas this is Ace. Ace this is my best friend, Chas."

I extended my hand to Chasity for a handshake and immediately noticed that she was hesitant to take it. Di was too giddy with excitement to even notice. "Ladi has told me a lot about you. For some reason, you look very familiar Chas. Have we met before?" I asked her.

"Chasity."

Taken aback I asked, "Excuse me?" "My name is Chasity so call me that."

Ladi who was first giddy was now somber. My once extended hand fell to my side because she never reciprocated my gesture. Grabbing two of her many bags to put in the car, I left her and Ladi standing there in a failed attempt to quietly bicker at one another.

"What was that about Chas? Why were you rude to him?"

"Girl I don't know him like that for him to be calling me Chas. You don't even know

"I do know him. You need..." before Ladi could finish her sentence, I was back grabbing

one of Chasity's suitcases and another bag.

After loading all of Chasity's three suitcases and four bags in my car, we made our way to Auntie Marie's house. The ride back was plagued with awkward silence with none us making an attempt to break it. The second I parked my car, I hurried to the trunk to take Chasity's luggage out and into the house. The more I thought about it, the more annoyed I was with how Chasity acted towards me. I wanted her out of my space as soon as possible. While I was unloading the car, Chasity was standing on the porch. Other than her purse, she didn't help with a single bag. Ladi, on the other hand, was still seating mutely in the passenger seat with the same grave expression she had when we first left the airport.

Once everything was unloaded, I walked over to the passenger side to help Ladi out of the car. I pulled Ladi into my arms and held her against me as I leaned on the side of the car. "Talk to me, mama."

She let out a heavy sigh and pressed her head into my chest. "Use your words, crazy girl." She tended to do that the more I got to know her. She would get so deep in her thoughts that she would lose her words - the same words that she highly valued. Ladi finally looked up at me, and I pulled her deeper into me. The heat that resonated from my body was a sure way to calm her down from the anxiety that was building up inside of her.

"I'm sorry for the way Chas acted towards you. That was not the reaction I was expecting from her. We've been talking about you for two weeks, and she seemed sincerely happy for me. Then she meets you and does that." Ladi began to shake her head, so I drew her even closer into me to calm her back down. "It's embarrassing baby." She whined.

"Do you have control over her actions?" I asked Ladi. Instead of answering she slowly shook her head no. This time I let her get away without using her words to answer me. "Then there isn't a reason for you to apologize for what she did."

Knowing firsthand the burden of always having to apologize for someone else's actions could have on a person, I tried to reason with Ladi. I had apologized for Sasha's actions several times in the past. It was exhausting, and I refused to let Ladi do that to herself.

"She was rude, but as long as she's a good friend to you, none of that matters to me." Bending over, I kissed her forehead, and she reacted by closing her eyes. I continued, "She looks familiar, but I don't know from where." I decided to get the subject out the way. Other than Saint being my brother, I couldn't hold anything else back from Ladi.

"She attended FIU too. We talked about that remember. Unless..." Her eyes grew wide with apprehension as she tried to jerk away from me.

"No. No. Hell no. I have never dealt with her in any way, I promise Di."

After laying her head back on my chest, she asked, "Then why are you adamant about
        knowing her?"

"I'm not adamant about it. I'm letting you know why I asked her if we met
        before."

"Oh." was the only response that came from Ladi.

"Take all those thoughts out of your mind. It's nothing like those crazy thoughts I know

you have running through your head right now." "Got it; they're gone."

Kissing her forehead again, I said, "I'm about to head to my first meeting. Will I be able to see you later?"

"Of course you will. When are you done with your last meeting?"

"Around five. If you're up for it, I wanted to take you and Chasity to dinner." If being around Chasity meant more time with Di, then it was something I was willing to do. Chasity gave me all types of bad vibes, but she was Ladi's best friend. I would have to be around her often - especially with her moving back to Miami - even though it wasn't something I cared to do at this point.

"You know that I am, but I have to talk to Chas about how she acted towards you first." "Understood. I'll text you when I make it." Allowing Ladi to finally remove herself

from me, she gave me one of her soft kisses that always took away my desire to do anything that

didn't involve me being in her company. She removed herself from my embrace, and we parted ways.

My first meeting after leaving Ladi was with Saint. When Ladi had mentioned that Chris acted like he owned Chez Saint, I knew that was a conversation that I had to have with Saint. It took me two days to bring it up to him because I was unsure if telling him was breaking Ladi's trust. Then I thought about the advances Chris made at her, and all rational thinking went out the window. It wasn't even the advances that bothered me the most. It was the way he treated her after she made it clear she wasn't interested that made my blood boil. Saint talked me out of confronting Chris. Ladi told me that he had been nothing but professional towards her since, which was the only thing saving him from me. Saint who had already suspected that he was abusing his authority was already in the process of taking care of it when I brought it up.

We had also spoken about him offering Ladi a better position than the one she had applied for. I felt stupid for thinking that I had something to do with it. And that's exactly how Saint had me feeling when I questioned him about it, stupid. He confirmed that Ladi got the

promotion based on her own merit. He saw how she could grow his business thus giving her the position he felt would most benefit Chez Saint.

Saint was outside playing with the twins when I made it to his driveway. I got out of the car, and both SJ and Heaven ran to me. They both were identical to Saint but had Angel's light complexion. Bending down, I picked one up in each arm. Saint approached me and offered me a head nod. I returned his welcoming gesture with a head nod of my own. Heaven began kissing me all over my face.

"You don't ever kiss daddy like that," Saint said pouting. His pout caused Heaven to start laughing as she reached out for him to grab her. Once she was in his arms, she started kissing all over his face. SJ must've gotten jealous because he reached out for Saint to grab him as well.

The second Saint reached out for him, he all but jumped out my arm. With the twins now in Saint's arms, we started walking towards the house. Watching Saint be a father for the past two years always had me longing for a family of my own.

Before walking in, I felt my phone vibrating. Figuring it was Ladi texting me, I waited until I was seated on his black leather recliner in the family room to get my phone out of my pocket. As I looked at Ladi's name on the screen, I couldn't stop the grin that formed involuntarily.

"When are you going to tell Ladi we're brothers Ace?" Saint asked causing my smile to

suddenly fall. Saint had been pressuring me for weeks to tell Ladi my relation to him.

"When the time is right," I said through gritted teeth.

"It's been a month since you started pursuing her bro." Nothing got under my skin more than when Saint stated the obvious.

"I know how long it's been. What's your point?"

"My point is, you need to tell her sooner than later. Especially since you told me she specifically asked if we were related."

Rubbing my hand down my face, I tried to calm myself down. I clicked on the notification to read the text instead of responding to Saint. It was tiring having the same conversation with him every other day. I quickly replied to Ladi then sat my phone on the armrest. "I'll tell her this week."

"You better or else I'm telling her. I can't keep acting like I don't know about ya'll Ace. She's my employee and a damn good one. I'm not trying to lose her. And I know you aren't trying to lose her."

"I'm not," I confirmed.

"So just tell her before I do." Angel entered the room, walking over to where Saint was sitting with the twins at his feet, cutting our conversation short. Saint snatched Angel into his lap and kissed her neck. Their exchange of affection caused me to miss Ladi. She had plans to spend

time with an old friend and Chasity while I was in meetings all day. Six o'clock couldn't get here

fast enough.

"You look, good babe," Saint said to Angel once he removed his face from her neck.

"Thank you, baby. I invited my friend over to give her a short tour of the house before we go out. I've been putting it off for weeks." Angel stood and picked up Heaven and SJ from the floor. "I'm going to feed them before I leave."

Once Angel was out of the room, we resumed our conversation. "All I'm saying is, I like Ladi for you bro. Don't mess it up." Saint telling me that he liked Ladi for me was a big deal. He didn't like any of the women I dated in the past, Sasha being the main one. Where my parents were indifferent towards Sasha, Saint despised her. Whenever Angel introduced me to her best friend Monica, I was afraid they were going to get a divorce. They argued about it almost every day because he felt that Monica wasn't any different than Sasha.

"Tonight. I'm telling her tonight." He simply nodded his head in approval and changed the subject. My first meeting with an actual client wasn't until one in the afternoon, so I decided to hang out with Saint until then. It was convenient since my client lived on his side of town. We discussed his move to open two more Chez Saints outside of Florida, the progress of my new house, and his upcoming plans for Angel's birthday.

Angel later returned to the room with a tray of sandwiches, chips, and two bottles of water. "I got the twins to take a nap. You should be able to get some work done while I'm out," she said as she sat the tray on the black coffee table.

As soon as she was done sitting the tray down the doorbell rang. "That must be her."

Angel said leaving out of the family room towards the all-white living room.

"Who's her friend?" I asked Saint. "Does it matter? You have Ladi."

I shook my head, "That's not why I asked. You know I'm not that type of guy. I've just never known Angel to have friends."

He shrugged his shoulders, "Me either. Apparently, it's someone she knew when she went to FIU. Between the twins, being a wife, and working part-time as a nurse, she has a lot on her plate. When she brought up hanging out with someone that wasn't Monica, I was too excited to even ask for details."

We both started laughing because of how true his statement was. Saint felt that Monica was using Angel. During the brief time Monica and I dated, he felt that she was using me as well.

Therefore, he hated every time Angel brought Monica around. But he would never tell her to stop hanging out with her unless she put Angel in harm's way.

Angel walked back to the family room accompanied by laughter and more than one different pattern of footsteps. Saint and I grabbed our sandwiches at the same time, but his immediately fell from his hand onto the black shag carpet as his eyes landed at the doorway. Him dropping the sandwich didn't cause me to look over at the doorway. His opened mouth didn't even take my attention away from my sandwich for more than a few seconds. Her voice did.

"Ace," Ladi said right above a whisper. Sitting there at a loss of words, I didn't know how to explain the reason I was sitting in Saint's house. I couldn't lie to her face and say it was only a business meeting. Hiding the truth was one thing but blatantly lying to Ladi was out of the question.

"What are you doing here Ace?" her soft voice was now shaky. My voice was stuck in my throat hindering me from finding the words to explain myself. My eyes shifted to Chasity who was standing next to her with a devious grin plastered on her smug face. She was getting pleasure from Ladi's confusion. I felt the color drain from my face. My throat became dry, delaying me from uttering a word to clear up Ladi's confusion. My legs were too weak to guide me to her.

"Ace why are you sitting there with Saint? Is this your business meeting?" Her voice shakier than before. Looking back to Saint I pleaded with my eyes for him to answer for me.

"How do you know my husband and brother in law?" Angel asked before Saint could answer on my behalf. There wasn't any hint of anger in her voice. Angel knew Saint would never disrespect their marriage by cheating on her. She looked over at me for an answer but every effort I made to speak failed.

"Your husband? Your brother in law?" Ladi finally broke the gaze she had on me to look at Angel. As soon as her eyes left mine, I felt my strength slowly coming back. I opened my mouth to speak, but still, nothing came out.

"Yes, Saint is my husband and Ace is his younger brother. How do you know them?" Ladi whipped her head around to face me just as I saw the tears threatening to fall from her eyes. Without saying anything, Ladi turned around and sped walk out of the room. Everyone was staring at me including Saint.

"Is anybody going to tell me what's going on?" Angel asked as she looked around the room. I needed to get to Ladi, but I had yet to regain the strength in my legs.

"I'm going to go check on my best friend," Chasity said while rolling her eyes. Hearing her words led all my strength to return. She needed to be as far away from Ladi as possible.

Saint must've caught on to her attitude because he looked at her with angry eyes while saying, "Nah. You're going to sit down on that couch." Looking over at me, he continued while pointing from me to the direction of the door, "You need to go handle that."

Chasity didn't move from the doorway, but that was the least of my concern. I had to fix this issue with Di. Finding my strength, I stood and took long strides towards the front door. When I made it outside, the sight of Ladi leaning on the hood of her car with tears falling down her beautiful chocolate face triggered me to momentarily lose my balance. I figured she would've been upset when she found out but not like this. If I had known this would've been the outcome, I would've told her when she asked.

As I sauntered to her, I felt myself becoming weak. The only thing I wanted to do was squeeze her. "Beauty," I said causing her to look up at me. When our eyes connected, I began pleading with her, "Please, let me explain."

"How...can...you..." she said between sniffles. Those were the only words that were able to escape her lips before she began to cry controllably.

I moved closer to her and drew her into me. Ladi didn't try to push me away. Instead she gave me access to pick her up. I picked her up bridal style and walked over to my car so that we could have the conversation in private. Something told me that Chasity would come outside. I put her down to open the door to the back seat for my car to get in. After she was situated, I quickly jogged over to the other side. Once inside I said, "Talk to me, mama."

The smile that I was hoping would appear never did. The

words I was dying to hear were never spoken. The look that I was longing for to give me courage never came. Instead, Ladi stared out the window. Feeling defeated, I chose to just lay everything out on the table. "Beauty, my intentions weren't to lie to you. Hiding the fact that Saint is my older brother was my way of getting you to give me a chance. My actions were wrong, but my intent was pure. I promise you that Beauty."

"Everyone is going to think my promotion was because of you." she finally said. "But it wasn't."

"I know that, but everybody else will think otherwise."

She was right, and it was up to me to take away her fear of possible rumors. "Ladi look at me please." She rapidly shook her head with her eyes never leaving the window. "Beauty please, you worked hard to be where you are. Saint sees how great you are at what you do. Shouldn't

that be all that matters?" I asked her.

"You lied to me, that matters more."

Technically I didn't lie; I hid the truth. Was I going to tell her that? No, I knew better. "My actions were wrong. But would we have gotten this far had I not hid that Saint is my brother?" She shook her head, and I said, "Use your words, crazy girl."

Groaning softly, she responded, "No we wouldn't have gotten this far."

"All I wanted was a fair chance with you Beauty. I had planned on telling you sooner, but then your aunt was hospitalized. The timing was never right. I definitely didn't want you finding out like this. Please forgive me Di."

As I waited for Ladi to answer me, she never looked up at me once. She didn't face me. She gazed out the car window the entire time. She had me feeling like I lost her just when I was falling for her. If I did lose her, I wouldn't have anyone to blame but myself. This just wasn't something I felt was worth losing her over. Yes, I hid something from her, but my intentions were good. It wasn't as if I lied about another woman or forced Saint to treat her differently because she and I were dating. I just needed to get Ladi to see it the way I did.

"Maybe Chasity was right," she mumbled thinking I didn't hear her. Her words punched all the air out of my lungs.

"Right about what?"

Silence.

"Right about what Di?" I could literally feel my anger building up. "What did she say about me after I left?"

Turning around she asked, "What does that have to do with anything Ace?" She attempted to turn back towards the window, but I stopped her. Refusing to let her shut me out, I grabbed her chin.

"Tell me what she said about me Beauty."

"She said that I don't know you. She stressed the point that I don't have much experience

with dating, but she did. She said that she could tell you weren't any good for me."

Shaking my head, I let Ladi's chin go, "What real reasons did she have to tell you these things Di?" She remained quiet, forcing me to answer for her, "Absolutely none. I messed up by hiding one thing from you. I'm guaranteeing that will never happen again. She shouldn't have a say to anything pertaining to us. She doesn't know me, but you do. I get that she's your best friend, just be careful. Can you do that for me?"

Before she could nod, I said, "Use your words, crazy girl." "Yes, I can do that for you."

"You forgive me Di?"

"Yes."

"Are you still mine?" I asked her. The smile that I was hoping for, finally came. It felt great to know that I still had the ability to make her smile.

"Forever," she answered. With that one word, all my emotions began to pour out freely.

There weren't any secrets between us. My guilt was gone. My Ladi had forgiven me.

"Forever." I leaned over and took her bottom lip into my mouth. Gently sucking on it hoping to bring as much pleasure as she needed to forget the pain that I had just brought to her.

As our kiss intensified, I grabbed Ladi by her waist for her to straddle me. She began to slowly grind on my growing manhood. Getting in the rhythm of her hips I began to match her movements. Ladi removed her lips from mine and ran her tongue up the side of my neck. She was finally ready for me.

I pulled Ladi's head back by her wild hair and began attacking her neck. Her moans blessed my ears with each wet lash of my tongue. I needed to taste her again. I had to feel her. Thankfully she was wearing a short, loose-fitting yellow sundress. Using my right hand, I pushed her panties to the side allowing her to release the puddle that was forming in between her legs onto my hand. Using my middle finger, I began rubbing on the most sensitive part of her body. The whimpers that left Ladi's lips were sensual and melodic. So sensual that I could've climaxed from the pleasure it brought to my ears. Her love sounds became louder as I watched her bite her bottom lip in ecstasy. The puddle was now a full-blown river. Switching fingers, I used my thumb to continue rubbing the spot that she was enjoying while using my middle finger to find the source of the river that was ever flowing.

There was no going back. The tightness that surrounded my finger left him wanting to feel her. What was his to have. What he had been patiently waiting for. As I felt Ladi's warm walls tighten around my finger, I said: "Talk to me, mama."

"I'm ready baby!" Ladi screamed as she reached her peak. Her words confirming what her body had already told me. As she came down from her high, I pulled my finger from her and sucked the nectar from it, my new addiction. Ladi grabbed my hand and licked the same finger that I had just removed from my mouth. My mouth dropped open as I watched her slowly lick my finger while never removing her eyes from mine. That was easily the sexiest thing I had ever witnessed.

Afterward I kissed her neck and rested my head there. "Ladi let's make us official."

I felt her move, but I pushed my head deeper into the crook of her neck not wanting to break our connection. The sweet smell of the Marc Jacob's Daisy perfume I had purchased for her, and her natural scent evaded my nose. "Are you asking me to be your girlfriend?" Her once sad voice was now filled with joy.

"Yes, Beauty. Will you be my girlfriend, my future wife, my forever?"

"Yes, baby, all of the above." I finally removed my head from her neck and kissed her

forehead. Her eyes closed instinctively.

"I promise to never hide anything from you again. You are an amazing woman Ladi.

Thank you for not fighting me."

"Thank you for being man enough to put actions behind your words. Every day since our redo date you've lived up to your words. You gave them meaning instead of turning them into broken promises."

"Forever."

"Forever," Ladi confirmed.

We sat in the car for a few more minutes going in depth as to why I withheld the information about Saint and I being brothers. She claimed to have forgiven me, but I wanted to make sure that she could really move past it. Rumors may spread. She needed to be ready for that. Wanting to do something special for her tonight, I got her to agree to go on a date with me alone. The fact that Chasity was speaking on a relationship she knew nothing about left a bad taste in my mouth. Eventually, I would have to be around her but not tonight.

After we were done talking and I was assured that she and I were on the same page, we walked back to the house. We made it to the family room to find Chasity still standing at the doorway while Saint and Angel were on the floor playing with the twins.

Saint gave me a concerned look as soon as we entered the family room. I nodded my head in response. Walking over to the recliner, I grabbed Ladi's hand to follow.

"I was telling Saint how I met Ladi," Angel said breaking the silence. She always had a way of lightening up the mood.

"Oh yeah?' I said with my eyes on Ladi.

"We had a class together my freshman year at FIU. She was also the nurse that found my aunt." Ladi never told me which hospital her aunt was in. If she had, I would've thought about the likelihood of her running into Angel. As Ladi and Angel reminisced on their friendship, Chasity had a hint of jealousy in her eyes.

"I'm hungry. Are we still going out to eat or no? The

conversation you all are having is not going to fill me up." Chasity reminded me of Sasha after she spoke those words. She was in my brother and sister in law's house being disrespectful. Not bothering to respond to her, I

leaned back into the recliner waiting for either Saint or Angel to put Chasity in her place. For the most part, Angel was soft-spoken, but she had been around Saint for so long, she began to have his ruthlessness. Saint, on the other hand, was Saint, and it didn't take much to set him off.

What I wasn't expecting was for Ladi to say anything, "Chas you can leave if you don't want to be here. No one is stopping you."

Chasity stood at the doorway with a shocked expression. Saint began laughing hysterically.

"I'm just hungry, that's all." That only caused Saint's laughter to grow louder. He always made a situation worse than it needed to be, this wasn't any different.

"I'm going to put the twins back down for a nap then we can go. Saint stop laughing and grab SJ for me." Angel said, and Saint stopped laughing immediately. She had a way of getting Saint to do any and everything. Now that I was with Ladi, I was finally able to understand it. The right woman would never make you feel like she was controlling. Instead, you'd be willing to do anything she asked because her happiness brought happiness into your life. I'd make a fool of myself to keep a smile on Ladi's face.

While Saint and Angel put the twins down for a nap, I guided Ladi towards the front door. Chasity was already outside waiting on them.

"Did I come off as rude?" Ladi asked as I drew her in for a hug.

"She was rude Di, not you."

"I just don't understand what her problem is. This isn't

the Chas I know. I mean, she's done a few petty things, but this is on another level. When I tried talking to her earlier all she could focus on is how you aren't good for me."

Letting go of Ladi's waist, I dragged my right hand down my face. That always seemed to help me calm down whenever I felt myself getting irritated. "Listen to me Di, don't let that girl get in your head. If she's a good friend like you say she is, then let it go. As far as you and I go, she doesn't need to speak on that."

"I hear you baby," she responded. I kissed her on her forehead before we parted ways. I watched as she walked outside to join Chasity. The last thing I wanted Ladi to think was that I was trying to dictate her friendship. My issue wasn't with her friendship, it was with her friend. It bothered me that Chasity felt the need to speak on our relationship.

"She's a good one," Angel said before rushing past me. I was so deep in my thoughts that I hadn't noticed her. Before I could respond, she was out the door.

"I'm in the all-white room!" Saint yelled as soon as Angel locked the door behind her.

When I arrived in the room, Saint had a bottle of Hennessy and two glasses on the table "Angel is going to catch you in here one day." I said shaking my head.

"You plan on telling her?" I didn't respond. "Exactly, she's never going to find out. Not trying to get in your business but are you and Ladi good?"

Saint really wasn't trying to get in my business. He was making sure I didn't mess up his. "Yeah, we're good. We made it official. It's only been a month, but she's the one."

"When you know, you know. I bought Angel's engagement ring after our second date." "The second date!" I exclaimed.

"You know that feeling you say you had when you first saw Ladi?" I remained silent but nodded my head so that he could continue, "That's the same feeling I had when I saw Angel. After two dates with her, I bought the ring. It took me five months to actually give it to her."

"When you know, you know," I confirmed.

❧ 14 ❧

ce

AFTER A DAY OF MEETINGS, I WAS EXHAUSTED. INSTEAD of taking Ladi out for dinner, we agreed for her to come over to my condo for the first time. Tonight was going to be a relaxing night since that's what she enjoyed the most. Lady was indecisive about what she wanted to eat which was why I ordered chicken wings. Seafood and wings were the two foods that Ladi would never turn down. As it got closer to six, I started to get nervous. A text from Ladi came through letting me know she was on her way up right when I started pacing back and forth.

The light knocks on my front door prompted my heart rate to increase. My nervousness stemmed from it being her first time at my condo. The planned surprise in my bedroom just amplified it. Taking a deep breath, I went to open the door for Ladi. She stood in front of me

146

with her hair in small individual twists, dark grey leggings, and one of my black t-shirts. She was so simple, so beautiful.

I moved to the side granting her access to enter. "No shirt and basketball shorts. You are

really in your element."

The smile that graced her beautiful chocolate face brought one to mine. "I'm always in my element when you're around Beauty," I responded stirring her away from the doorway and into the living room.

"This place is you," she said as she turned around to face me. "Should I say thank you?" I asked unsure how to respond.

She gave me one of her signature smiles, "Yes, that was a compliment. Just like you could tell a lot about me from my room, I can say the same about your condo. You are definitely a minimalist. That's a good thing."

"In that case, thank you Beauty."

"You're welcome, baby. Where can I put my overnight bag?" I hadn't even noticed the bag in her hand. She shook her head, "I'm sorry, I didn't even ask if it was ok for me spend the night."

Taking the bag from her, I said, "You don't have to apologize crazy girl. I miss you squeezing your little body under me. The past few nights have been restless without you."

"Thank goodness!" she let out a heavy sigh. "I needed to hear you say that. The nurse is staying overnight with my aunt. Is it ok if I get ready for work here in the morning?"

"Sounds perfect. Make yourself at home Di. I'm going to put your bag in the bedroom. The remote and wings are on the coffee table."

That gorgeous smile slowly crept across her face again, "What flavor did you get?" "Your favorite, honey chipotle."

"They're your favorite too." Ladi ate honey chipotle wings at least twice a week. She didn't want to share her food with me at first. When she finally did give me a wing to try, honey chipotle became my new favorite flavor.

"Yeah, whatever crazy girl. There's lemonade in the fridge. Just get comfortable. I'll be right back."

I turned around and headed down the hallway towards the direction of my bedroom. I placed Ladi's bag in the closet, stopping to prepare her surprise, and grabbed the small box that was on top of my dresser. Initially, I wanted to wait and give it to her at the end of the night, but the sight of her made me change my mind.

With my hand behind my back, I returned to the living room. Ladi was sitting with her legs crossed on the floor with her back against the longer side of the sectional. The plate of wings was in her lap. She was more concentrated on her plate than the TV that she had turned on. It was crazy to think how close we had gotten this past month. That closeness, the comfortability were things I never wanted us to lose. She was sitting on my floor while wearing my t-shirt with a plate of chicken wings in her lap, still looking as stunning as when she dressed up for one of our many outings.

I sat down next to her, "Why did you turn the TV on if you weren't going to watch it?"

"You said to get comfortable. Comfortable means that the TV is on. Doesn't mean I have to
watch it."

"That's one of the many reasons I call you crazy girl." She used her small body to nudge me. No matter how hard she tried, Ladi was never able to physically move me. I was big in stature but compared to her, I was a giant.

Pulling the small box from behind me I said, "I got you something Beauty."

She put the plate to the side of her, wiped her hands, and turned around to face me. As soon as I opened the box, her eyes grew big. "These charms are also from Pandora's Essence Collection. Each one represents an element in our relationship."

Ladi took the bracelet off her wrist as I removed the first charm. It was deep purple and round with small triangular designs. "This is the peace charm. The reason I'm giving you this is because that's what you brought to me when I least expected it but needed it the most."

She took it from my hand, permitting me to remove the second one from the box - a light gray circular charm. "This is the balance charm. We bring balance to each other. Without you by my side, my life feels unsteady Di. We nourish each other. We support one another. We are different but the same. We are each other's center."

Before taking the last one out of the box, I wiped away the tears that were freely rolling down her cheeks. Trying to finish what I had to say, I cleared my throat. The last round charm was white with a silver line that ran down it vertically. "This is the honesty charm. Ladi, I am vowing to always be honest with you. After what happened today, seeing the pain that my dishonesty caused you, I promise to never keep anything from you."

This time I took the bracelet from her, adding the last charm on it myself. Kissing her wrist, I placed the bracelet back on. Ladi wore the bracelet every day. At times, I would even catch her admiring each charm individually. Knowing the value that words held was the reason I began giving Ladi the charms. Each represented a word that my actions would prove to her daily.

"Thank you, baby." Ladi kissed my lips with an urgency that I had never felt before.

"Can we go to the bedroom?" she asked after removing her soft lips from mine.

Without saying a word, I stood up and extended my hand to help her to her feet. Our hands entwined as I led Ladi to my bedroom. Ladi released my hand before entering into the room. There were scented candles that lined the room. The once dark room was now dimly lit by the glow of the many candles that I lit before returning to the living room. It was filled with the sweet scent of lavender and French vanilla. Ladi walked around with her hands covering her mouth. No longer able to withstand the space between us, I strolled over to her.

As I drew her into me by her waist, I began laying tender kisses on every inch of her face. Our lips connected as I lifted Ladi into the air. She wrapped her thick but toned legs around my waist. Using my hands to keep her in place, I laid her in the center of my king size bed that was decorated with coral colored rose petals. I broke our connection in order to situate myself at the edge of the bed to get a full view of her

"What's the significance of the coral?"

Before answering, I removed my basketball shorts and my boxer briefs. "Desire."

The lust in Ladi's eyes prompted my manhood to rise. Stroking him, I watched as Ladi began to remove her clothes. Tonight would be the first time we made love, although I had tasted Ladi countless times. Her honied nectar was my drug.

"Look in the first drawer of the nightstand."

Doing as she was told, Ladi opened the drawer and took out the piece of paper." Without reading it, she asked, "What's this baby?"

"Read it, crazy girl." I chortled at the thought that had it been anyone else asking me the

obvious, I would've been annoyed. Yet with Ladi, it made me laugh.

"Your results to an STD test? You already gave me one a couple of weeks ago."

"I know, but this is going to be our first time making love. I made sure to get another one because I don't want anything separating us. There are many components to trust. Never will I put any part of you in harm's way. Your mind, your soul, your body, and your heart. You can trust me with all of you."

After returning the paper to the nightstand, Ladi seductively crawled towards where I was standing at the edge of the bed. Replacing my hand with her small hand, it barely wrapped

around my shaft as she began stroking it. My mouth opened and closed from the pleasure of her soft hands going up and down slowly. Soft moans fled from my lips as her warm mouth wrapped around the tip. The more she took in her mouth, the harder it was to control my breathing. Her

full lips were mesmerizing as they went from the tip almost to the base. My body wouldn't permit my eyes to close. The satisfaction from watching Ladi command my body with just her warm lips and wet tongue transported me to a state of euphoria. In the past week, Ladi had learned how to orally please me effortlessly.

My breathing slowed down as her paced increased. Her saliva coating my manhood almost brought me to my breaking point. All I wanted was to be inside of her. "Lay back for me Di." She did as I said, and the detachment had me needing her more than air. "Spread your legs for me."

Ladi immediately spread her legs at my demand. As

badly as I wanted to devour her to get my dose of drug, the need to feel her around me was excruciating. Positioning myself in the middle of her legs, Ladi began running her hands down my back. "I'm ready baby."

"This may hurt a little at first, but you'll feel good afterward. I'll go slow." Ladi hungrily attacked my lips, and I reciprocated that same hunger. The wetness flowing in between Ladi's thighs gave me access to enter her with more ease than I was expecting. Her tightness had a strong grip on the couple inches of my ten inches that I was able to get in. Slowly, I began to move my hips in a circular motion. The wetter she became, the more I was able to fill her up.

The dimly lit room was now filled with Ladi's loud moans and whimpers. To keep myself from groaning out loud, I pressed my head in the crock her neck. Only removing it to say, "I'm falling for you Beauty."

Finally, filling her up completely, an animalistic growl escaped from my throat. My slow circular motions turned into hard, powerful thrusts. Ladi's nails glided down my back with every thrust of my pelvis into her. This soul tie solidified it for me. I was falling in love with Ladi. We were in sync. Our connection was organic and untainted. We were undoubtedly forever.

15

Ladi

THE PAST COUPLE OF MONTHS HAD BEEN NOTHING short of eventful. My relationship with Ace was strong. We had our differences but what couple didn't? My aunt's health was improving, but she hadn't started back working. We disagreed about her returning, but there wasn't anything stopping her. Thankfully, she decided only to work part-time. Working at Chez Saint was everything I expected it to be. Stressful but in a good way. I was putting my degrees to use and getting great experience.

The rumor of Ace being the reason I received my position spread like wildfire just as I knew it would. I worked harder to prove that I deserved my position. Saint didn't offer me any special treatment, so he watched me go above and beyond without as much as saying a word. Chris made it worse than it had to be. He prolonged the rumor way after Saint himself shut it down. It got to the point that Ace came to my job to confront him. It was embarrassing, to say the least, but Ace felt that it was necessary. Since then, everything had gone back to normal for the most part.

"Can you believe Kenny hasn't reached out to me?" "Do you want him to reach out to you?"

"Yes. I mean no. He cheated on me with two different women and impregnated them both. The least he could do is call to check in on me Ladi. It's been over a month since I moved

back."

Not knowing what to say to Chas, I simply shrugged my shoulders. We were having lunch at Seven Seas Restaurant in Little Haiti. They had the best Cape Cod chicken salad. Unlike everything else, our friendship wasn't progressing. As my friendship with Angel grew, ours appeared to be diminishing. It wasn't deliberate, but Chasity had negative energy that I didn't care to be around. She saw negative in everything. I ignored it for as long as I could because she was my best friend. Now, it was almost agonizing.

"Ace has changed you," Chas said causing me to let out a deep sigh. I sunk lower in my chair preparing myself for a conversation we had every other day since I told her Ace and I had made our relationship official.

"He has changed me Chas but not in the way you make it out to be." "Then how is it? I don't even know my best friend anymore."

"You keep saying that, but you are never able to explain why you feel that way," I stated. Ace did change me, but it was for the better. He showed me how to make myself a priority. Not only that, he showed me how to have fun. For most of my life, all I did was work and go to school. I never stepped out of my comfort zone. Ace pretty much pushed me out of it and made

me enjoy the one life I had to live. He balanced me, we really were each other's center. Chasity just didn't have the ability to grasp that concept.

She rolled her eyes. "All we ever talk about is Ace."

"That's because you choose to always bring him up, Chas." Ace and I weren't one of those couples that allowed our relationship to consume us. We had set boundaries for one another. Both of us made time for our relationship and those around us.

"And why is that Ladi? He's going to have you looking stupid. I know his type." "His type? Why can't you believe that he is genuinely a good guy?"

"You don't know him!" she shouted. Dealing with Chas was draining. It was always the same conversation. She felt that Ace wasn't good for me but could never offer a valid reason as to why she felt that way. I ignored her as much as I could, but it was getting out of hand. My aunt had mentioned that it could've been jealousy. She was my best friend, so I didn't want to believe it.

"Chas drop it, please. You are my best friend, so I'm saying this in the politest way for the

last time, your opinion about Ace isn't needed."

Waving her hands back and forth, Chas replied, "You don't have to tell me all but once." That was a lie. This had to be at least my sixth time telling her to not speak on Ace. He didn't give her any reason to doubt him. I wasn't going to let her cloud my judgment either. That is where a lot of women made a mistake. They would let their friends' opinions interfere with their romantic relationships. There's a difference in asking a friend for advice and allowing her to bash your significant other.

"Anyway, I really appreciate you for vouching for me with Saint."

"You did all that yourself. No need to thank me because if you weren't any good Saint would not have hired you." Chasity had been working as a bottle girl at Chez Saint's lounge for a little over a week. She was good at what she did, so my position didn't help her get the job.

"I know but still. Staying at your aunt's house this long wasn't a part of my plan. I appreciate her for letting me stay there. It's just time for me to get my own place and I'll be able to do that soon with the money I'm making. Plus you are always at Ace's condo."

My voice heightened, "Chas, what did I just say?" She threw her hands up in surrender and took a sip of her water. Ace and I did spend a great deal of time together, but we also gave each other space. I spent two nights at his place a week. On my off days, I would bring him

lunch at his office. He made sure to take me out for date night once a week. However, we gave each other time to spend with the other people in our lives. Our relationship was new, but it didn't define us. Ace explained to me that it was imperative that we knew how to have friendships and relationships outside of our own.

"Since you have Ace, I may go for Saint," Chasity stated causing me to start choking on my water.

"What? You know he's married to Angel."

"What's your point? Divorces happen every day." The seriousness in her voice made me shake my head.

"You are joking right?" Chasity offered me a playful smirk, but her eyes said it all. The truth was evident in her silence. "Chas you better not try anything with Saint. Angel is our friend."

"Correction, she's your associate. You and I are friends. But Saint is off limits, got it."

Instead of correcting her, I continued to eat my food. Everything didn't warrant a response, and at that moment, I decided to move past all of Chasity's negativity. When she realized I wasn't going to say anything she changed the subject. "My sister reached out to me earlier this week. While you hang out with Angel, I'll go see her."

Chasity having family wasn't new information but her actually spending time with them was. She never met her dad or his side of the family. Once he found out that her mom was pregnant, he left her high and dry. Chasity's mom resented her because she thought that having a child by a rich white lawyer would guarantee her place in his life. She lived in denial that she would be more to him than what she actually was to him: a mistress.

Every chance her mom could, she treated her poorly because Chasity was her biggest mistake. To my knowledge, Chasity and her older sister didn't have much of a relationship either. Other than the little bit of her past she told me, I didn't know much about her family. No names, no faces, nothing.

"Wow, that's really good."

She shrugged her shoulders and said, "It is what it is."

We continued with small talk for the duration of our lunch. Afterward, Chasity left to go meet with her sister and I headed to Angel's house. She had asked me to meet with her to help with planning her birthday celebration.

After ringing the doorbell, I waited for Angel to come to the door. Angel swung the door open with a huge grin. She reached for my hand before leading me into the family room.

"Thank you for coming on such short notice." She said once she was seated on one end of the love seat.

I sat on the other end and responded, "It's no big deal. Today is my day off, and I didn't have anything else planned."

"Well, I appreciate it either way. My best friend was supposed to help me plan it, but she

canceled last minute."

"Believe me I do not mind at all. So why is that you're planning your birthday celebration again? You had mentioned that Saint always goes over and beyond for you."

"He does, and that's why I'm planning it this year." The look of confusion that I offered impelled her to continue, "I see that I'm confusing you, so I'll explain, but this has to stay between us."

"You have my word."

"I'm fourteen weeks pregnant. Saint doesn't know yet. My plan is for us to celebrate my birthday in St. Lucia with his family. We all know that he's going to give me an elaborate party. What he won't know is that it's going to be a surprise to announce the new baby to him. That's where you come in."

Angel's smile caused one to tug at the corners of my lips. Moving closer, I gave her a hug. "Congratulations Angel. I am so honored you trust me to help you plan this."

Her body began to jerk, and she broke our embrace allowing me to see that she was in tears. "I'm sorry for being emotional," she said wiping her face with both of her hands. "After having the twins, I had to get one of my ovaries removed. When the doctor told me that it would be difficult for me to have more children, I watched my husband's heart literally break. We suffered three miscarriages since then.

Each time, it took something from him that I'm unable to replace."

She took my hands and placed them on her stomach. Angel was a naturally curvy plus size woman. Her stomach wasn't flat, but she had a slim waist for her size. If she hadn't told me she was pregnant, I wouldn't have guessed it. "This baby is a fighter. All three miscarriages ended before I was even eight weeks. This is our miracle."

I listened tentatively as she spoke, "Saint isn't perfect, but he is the most loving man I know. He cherishes me with everything in him. The miscarriages hurt us both, but he remained strong for me. He mourned the loss of our babies while watching me in pain. Giving him this surprise means everything to me."

The tears that were fighting to be released began to fall freely. "Thank you for letting me

be a part of the planning. You have to make sure Ace records it for me."

Wiping the last of her tears, Angel cleared her throat, "What do you mean make sure Ace

records it for you? You're going to be there."

Both Angel and Ace had mentioned the trip to St. Lucia for Angel's birthday. As much as I wanted to go, Ace had to be the one to tell me that I was going to be there. His parents were in St. Lucia, and he may not have been ready for me to meet him. "If Ace wants me there, I'll be there."

Angel began laughing and pulled her phone out of the back pocket of her jeans. "Oh, he wants you there. Watch and see." She sat the phone on the coffee table that was in front of us, went through her contacts list, and tapped on Ace's name.

The phone rang three times before he answered. His deep voice instantly took me to a place of tranquility. "Hey sis, what's going on?" "I needed to ask you something."

"Ask." I shook my head at his short his response. He was definitely on his way to a meeting.

"Since my birthday is coming up in three weeks, I'm trying to finalize my guest list for

Saint. Are you still planning on bringing Ladi?"

The only thing that could be heard in the room was the faint thumping of my heart in my chest while we waited for Ace's answer. After a short pause, he let out a long grunt. "Yes, already booked her ticket. Just need to talk to her first."

"Ok, got it." Angel quickly said before hanging up the phone. The look on her face was confirmation that I wasn't supposed to hear that. Before I could ask her any questions, she held her hand up to stop me.

"Don't ask because I'm not sure what he needs to talk to you about. Just wait and hear

him out."

I wasn't sure what Ace wanted to talk to me about, but it felt good to know that he wanted me there with him. Waiting was my only option, Angel made it clear I wasn't going to get any information from her.

"I MISSED YOU TODAY BEAUTY." ACE SAID BARELY above a whisper. Wrapping me tighter in his arms, Ace laid a kiss my forehead. We had just gotten back from our date night and were now laying down in bed at his condo.

"I missed you too." The entire night my mind kept going back to the conversation between him and Angel. Our date was a helicopter ride over South Beach which didn't leave much room for conversation. Now that we were out the shower and in bed, I kept wondering when he was going to finally bring it up.

"We need to talk Di." Just like that my body tensed up and I tried to remove myself from his tight hold. He let me go, and I sat down on my knees so that I could look at him. The room was faintly lit by the scented candles that I added to his room enabling me to see his muscular silhouette on the bed.

Without meaning to, I held my breath waiting for him to begin. Nothing good ever followed we need to talk. Ace's deep laughter filled the entire room, "Breath crazy girl." I slowly let out a breath which led to him laughing irrepressibly.

After he regained his composure, he continued. "Look, I want you to come to St. Lucia with me for Angel's birthday celebration. My parents know about you and can't wait to meet you. However, there is something you have to know..."

"What is it?" I asked cutting him off.

"Monica."

"Who is Monica?"

"Angel's best friend. She and I dated for a couple of months. She's going to St. Lucia as well for the birthday celebration. It wouldn't be fair for me to ask Angel to make her not come. If you aren't comfortable being around her, we can stay here and go another time." When he finished,

he waited for me to respond. Monica had every right to be there to celebrate with Angel. I wasn't aware of his past with her, but that's exactly what it was. A past.

"Do you still have feelings for her?" Without hesitation, he answered, "No." "Are you confident in what we have?"

He lifted himself up by his elbows so that he was closer to my face. "Very, Beauty."

"Then there isn't an issue with her being there. Your past doesn't intimidate me. It

doesn't cause me to have any doubts about what we have. Only your actions can do that."

No sooner than my last word fell from my lips, Ace sent his crashing onto mine. Our tongues entangled as he used his hands to guide me closer to him. He was aggressive and passionate. My words had satisfied a hunger that he seemed to have had all day from not knowing how I would feel by Monica accompanying us to St. Lucia. I had just given him the affirmation he needed to feed that hunger.

"I'm falling hard for you Di," he whispered onto my lips. The sweetness of his words left me speechless for a second. Was this the love that I had been missing my whole adult life? I never ran from it, but it never came either. Was Ace the only person that could lead me through my journey of love?

I knew the answer as soon as I said, "I'm falling for you too."

❦ 16 ❦

 ce

AFTER OFFICIALLY DATING FOR THREE MONTHS, I WAS finally taking Ladi to meet my family back in St. Lucia. I'd only known Ladi for four months total, but I couldn't imagine my future without her. She offered me a sense of security that was unwavering. It's crazy how you never knew how

much you needed something until you had it. With Ladi, there wasn't any doubts about what we were or where we were going. She didn't leave any room for me to have any insecurities because she didn't have any. We weren't perfect, but we were the closest thing to it in my eyes.

The only thing that could ruin this moment for me was the fact that Monica was going to be on this trip with us. Ladi assured me she didn't have any concerns, but I couldn't erase the nagging feeling in the back of my mind. Putting

Ladi in an uncomfortable position with another woman from my past was the last thing that I wanted. I was just praying that Monica would be an adult about that situation. The five-day trip was to celebrate Angel's twenty-sixth birthday, but it was also Ladi's introduction to my entire family.

My family's approval of Ladi wasn't obligatory because my heart was all in. Nothing could change that. However, I valued Ladi, and that meant that she deserved to meet the most important people in my life. Saint was team Ladi which meant my parents would be too. It was more of a formality since nobody's opinion could sway me in any other direction than where I was already headed with Ladi.

Saint and I were now sitting in the terminal at Miami International Airport waiting for Ladi and Angel to return from getting food. Monica and Angel's cousin from Tennessee, Harmony, were on their way to the airport to meet us so that we could all fly out together.

"You ready for Ma and Pops to meet Ladi?" Saint asked. He had a ridiculous sneer on his

face.

"Take that goofy smile off your face. Yeah, I'm ready."

"You have nothing to worry about honestly. They'll love her bro."

"I'm not worried because even if they didn't, that wouldn't change anything for me." "That's exactly how I felt about Angel. Ma hated the age difference, but I didn't let that

stop me from being with who my heart chose. Eight years later she's still my reason for breathing. She gave me purpose the moment she entered my life. Her giving me the twins completed me. I want that for you Ace."

I nodded my head listening to my older brother speak. It

was one of the rare moments where he wasn't joking. "I appreciate it for real man."

Changing the subject, I asked, "Why are we staying in Castries instead of Gros Islet?" My parents had homes in both St. Lucia's capital Castries and our hometown Gros Islet. Both houses were beautiful two-story traditional St. Lucian homes. Castries had more things to do, but I preferred the atmosphere of Gros Islet. It was just as beautiful and not as busy as Castries.

"Since Monica and Harmony are going to be there, Ma felt that Castries would be better with it being more touristy."

As soon as I was getting ready to respond, the sight of Monica stopped my words from forming. I watched as she trotted over trying my best to pick up on her aura. Saint had mentioned that Angel had told her about Ladi. Unfortunately, that didn't give me much confidence that Monica wouldn't make this difficult.

She and I hadn't spoken in close to nine months. It had been well over nine months since we last saw each other. Monica was a beautiful woman. Her light brown hair was cut into a short bob. She was short with very wide hips. She wouldn't be considered plus-sized, but she wasn't small either. Based on the three women that I had recently dated, you could tell I didn't have a type. Certain features looked better on certain women. I was attracted to beauty. Every woman defined beauty differently.

Our eyes stayed connected the entire time she walked towards us. I could feel Saint burning a hole on the side of my face. He had nothing to worry about because I felt no emotional connection to Monica. Our eye contact was confirmation of that. Staying clear of her the entire trip to avoid her bringing up our past was the only plans I had for us.

"Ace, it feels so good to see you." Monica's wide grin took over her oval shaped face. The light in her eyes slowly darkened out when she realized that I wasn't going to return the same enthusiasm.

"Monica. Harmony." I nodded my head to acknowledge both women. Standing up, I dragged my hand down my face as I headed in the direction that Ladi and Angel had left in earlier.

Being friendly wasn't going to make the situation any less uncomfortable. It would only complicate it. There was no way that I was going to leave any room for my friendliness to be misinterpreted as something more than what it was. If it meant that I had to give Monica the cold shoulder, then that was exactly what I was going to do.

Ladi never asked, but Monica and I did have a sexual relationship. As badly as I wanted to tell her, she didn't allow me to. She kept saying that it was in the past and that's where it should stay. The more I thought about it, the more I began regretting my decision to go on this trip. Angel was my sister, but Ladi was my heart. If missing this trip would protect her feelings than that's what I should've done.

"Where are you going?" Turning around, I realized that I had walked past Ladi and Angel. I really needed to get out of my head.

"To find you. What took you all so long?"

"Someone wanted to be indecisive," Ladi said eyeing Angel causing them both to burst out in laughter. I loved seeing Ladi relaxed like this. She had on a short olive t-shirt dress with a pair of white converses. Her hair was loose in the wild mane that I admired. The way she could switch up her style so effortlessly always made me smile.

"I see. Who is all that food for? The flight isn't that long Angel."

"It's for all of us." She stated and walked off. Ladi stood there, and I couldn't help but to tug her into me so that I could wrap my arms around her small frame.

The moment she was against my chest, she looked up at me with her beautiful almond shaped eyes. I bent down and kissed her forehead. "Monica is here." was all I could manage to say.

With the utmost sincerity in her voice, she said, "We are solid. I'm not an insecure woman. We are not insecure people."

Simply nodding my head, I placed my lips on hers. There weren't any more words to be spoken amongst us. The uneasiness I had been feeling was starting to be replaced with certainty. After peeling her body from mine, Ladi grabbed my hand. We walked hand-in-hand to meet back up with everyone else.

When we made it back, the first thing I noticed was Saint's grim facial expression. It had to be because Monica was there. He openly did not like her. Saint sat across from the three women while they were deep in conversation. Angel looked up finally seeing us. She quickly stood up and grabbed Ladi's hand to yank her to where the other women were sitting. I went over to take a seat next to Saint. We were within hearing distance; therefore we were able to hear parts of their conversation. Angel was trying her best to include Ladi in the conversation, but as

expected, Monica was being standoffish. Ladi didn't let it get to her and appeared unbothered by

Monica's coldness. As if it were even possible, I respected her even more for that.

"I told Angel not to invite that girl," Saint said in a harsh tone making no effort to lower his voice. Everyone heard him but knew better than to say anything.

Unlike Saint, I was indifferent towards Monica. I just hated the fact that she had to be here in my presence with Ladi. The bad feeling that I had before slowly began to creep back. No matter how much Ladi reassured me she was ok, I couldn't seem to shake it off.

We sat around for close to thirty more minutes conversing and eating the food that Ladi and Angel had brought. As soon as they called for first class to board, we all stood up. Saint paid everyone's ticket but mine and Di's. He offered of course, but I declined since I had my own reasons for this trip as well.

The flight felt shorter than it was. Ladi slept the entire three hours and every minute of those three hours Monica kept her eyes on me. It was infuriating having to be around her because I just knew she was going to find a way to get into Ladi's head even if I refused to let it happen.

My parents' home wasn't too far from George F. L. Charles Airport, so instead of having them pick us up, Saint decided on renting a car. The St. Lucian sunshine was different than that of Miami. It was completely different from Tennessee's weather. The air was clear, the sun was bright, the island vibe was calming. Having Ladi by my side would only make the experience that much better.

Once we were all in the six-passenger SUV, Saint drove to our parent's house. Due to traffic, it took thirty minutes to get there. The gate opened, and Saint drove up the short driveway. My mom and dad were already outside waiting for us. My dad was tall and dark like myself and Saint. We both got our large frame as well as our physical features from him. He and Saint were the same height. My mom was tall as well with a smooth cocoa skin complexion. Other than her calm demeanor, I didn't inherit anything from her.

My mom didn't wait for us to get out of the car before she ran to it trying to open Saint's door. Between the two of us, Saint was a mama's boy. Other than Angel, she was the only other person that could talk sense into him.

"My boy!" She screamed as soon as Saint stepped out of the car. She wrapped her arms around him while we all stood around watching their embrace. My mom had a St. Lucian accent, but depending on who she was speaking with, it would change. Today, it was in full effect.

"I'm here too Ma," I said walking over to her. Everyone laughed as she held on to Saint's

hand while simultaneously dragging me in for a hug. My mother was the most nurturing woman

I had ever met. Our father taught us how to be men, but she taught us how to love.

After everyone was out of the car, my mother began greeting them all accordingly. When she got to Ladi, she gave her the longest hug. She said something to my father in St. Lucian Creole. When Ladi responded to her in Haitian Creole, she had the brightest smile on her face. The two languages were very similar. My parents made sure Saint and I spoke it. Angel had learned it and could hold a conversation. I made sure to leave out the part about Ladi being half Haitian to my mom so that I could see that smile on her face. Ladi was winning her over just as I expected.

Soon after everyone properly greeted my parents, we all went to our respective rooms to get some much-needed rest. We would all be having a late lunch that my mom prepared for all of us. Since this was our first day in town, we decided today would be a chill day. Tomorrow would be our day out. Angel's birthday was on the third day so that was when her party would take place. The last full day of our trip, Ladi and I were going to have our alone time so that I could give her a surprise.

As if she hadn't slept on the plane, Ladi fell back asleep after her shower. She was laying on her stomach with both of her arms tucked tightly underneath her body. Her hair, all over the place. Legs sprawled out. She was simply beautiful.

The soft knock on the door forced me to take my eyes away from Ladi. Opening the door, I found Saint on the opposite side of it with a scowl on his face. I quickly step outside, making sure to close the door behind me. If Ladi needed rest, I didn't want to interrupt her.

"What's wrong?" "Monica. She has to go."

Instead of agreeing with him, I waited for him to continue. "I've been watching her this whole time Ace. Her vibe is completely off. You can just tell she's itching to start something. When Ma and Ladi were speaking in Creole, she started steaming. Like, I real life saw steam coming from her ears."

Saint's straight-face forced a chortle from me. "Angel wants her here Saint. We both have to respect that. As long as it's not affecting Ladi, I can ignore it."

"Well, I can't. As soon as she says or does something stupid, she's gone. Angel already knows this. Apparently, they had a talk, and Monica said she would be cool. Her actions are showing different though."

Even though I was already feeling uneasy, I couldn't let Monica occupy any space in my mind with her negative energy. What she and I had was brief. Neither one of us were in love. She walked away and then later changed her mind. It was over nine months ago. There was nothing there to hold on to.

Saint reminded me what time lunch was going to start and left. Being that I had a couple of hours, I decided to cuddle under Ladi before we had to meet everyone else.

LUNCH WAS GOING BETTER THAN I ANTICIPATED. Everyone was laughing and enjoying themselves. My dad told the story of how he met my mom after Saint shared his story on his first encounter with Angel. It was still unbelievable that he bought an engagement ring after their second date.

When it was my turn to share, I was a little diffident. The only thing I wanted to remember about when I first saw Ladi was the instant connection that we shared. Everything else could be forgotten. Right before I could say anything, Monica said, "You should tell them how we met first since we did meet first." Her sneer was sadistic. She wore it proudly as if she was going to receive a reward.

The laughter that had once filled the room was now void. The only thing left was blank expressions. Ladi shifted in her seat which I assumed was because she was uneasy. My parents didn't know about mine and Monica's history, but now they did. After dinner, they were definitely going to have something to say.

"Will you all excuse us please?" Angel asked breaking the deafening silence that besieged the room. Monica was sitting next to her but directly across from me. In the past, it wasn't possible for me to detest another woman more than I detested Sasha until that very moment. Angel yanked her from her seat and hauled her out of the room with all her force.

I squeezed Ladi's thigh, and she offered me a weak smile in return. She was doing her best to keep it together. "I'm fine," she whispered so that only I was able to hear her. Her eyes told a different story. Ladi's eyes would never betray me. They could never lie to me. As I stared into her light brown eyes, I saw the embarrassment that stained them. She wasn't fine.

Monica and Angel never returned to the table. The dinner ended in the silence that Monica created. After we were done eating, my parents asked to speak to both Saint and me alone. Ladi and Harmony left the four of us at the table. My mom spoke first. She was disappointed that Ladi was put in that position, but she was furious that I didn't make them aware of my history with Monica. I then explained to them that our history was brief and ended with us no longer having contact with one another months prior to my pursuit of Ladi. Saint came to my defense which only made my dad chastise him for not being able to get Angel to see Monica's true intentions.

The minute they were done talking to us, I retired to my room to find Ladi sitting cross-legged at the edge of the bed. She was now in one of my t-shirts that swallowed her. Her wild mane-like hair was pulled into a high bun at the top of her head. She was so deep in her thoughts that she didn't even acknowledge me when I walked in.

Making my way over to her, I kneeled down in front of her. Taking her hands into mine, I

brought them to my lips and gently kissed them. "Talk to me, mama."

She closed her eyes and as each word fled her soft round lips, my heart rate increased, "You cannot control her words or her actions nor do I expect you to. It's just that," she paused as I held my breath waiting for her to finish "what we have is so pure. No matter what, I refuse to let it be tainted by your past when you are presently showing me that I am your future. Other women may have had you before me. That doesn't bother me because I am your forever

Ace."

The breath that I was holding came out in a soft groan. Did I really deserve the beautiful human that sat in front of me? Did I truly deserve this peace that she brought me while in her presence? At that moment, I vowed to spend every day we had together to show her that I did.

"You are my forever Beauty.

❧ 17 ❧

Ladi

TODAY WAS ANGEL'S BIRTHDAY, AND SAINT SPARED NO expense to make sure she felt special. The twins were flown in with their hired nanny. She begged to have them here for her birthday even though the party was an adult party. Little did Saint know, they were part of the surprise to announce her pregnancy to him. He had a chef come to prepare breakfast for us girls. Yes, Monica was still on the trip with us. After breakfast, we all went to get manicures and pedicures. When we returned home, four masseuses waiting for us to give us each a full body massage.

"I know it's your birthday Ang, but I feel like it's mine too." Harmony said bringing us all to laughter. We were currently having lunch prepared by the chef in the dining room of Ace's parents' home in our plush white robes. Harmony was a sweet girl. She reminded me so much of

Angel. If they didn't tell you they were cousins, you would've thought they were sisters. Not only did they favor but they acted alike.

"Ace took me to get a couple's massage once. Has he taken you to get one Ladi?"

Monica asked followed by a slick smirk.

Up until this point Monica had been on her best behavior. Ace had informed me that Angel threatened to make her leave after the stunt she pulled our first night in St. Lucia. Now, she was hoping for a reaction that I wasn't going to give her. Both Angel's and Harmony's mouth dropped open due to disbelief. I had been around Monica enough to know that she was waiting on the perfect opportunity to get under my skin.

"Actually no. I guess he opted to take me on a helicopter ride over South Beach instead."

My smile to her was genuine. My statement, however, was most certainly a jab.

"Oh. That's nice too. Woman to woman be careful with Ace. That ex of his ruined us.

You don't want the same thing to happen to you."

If I were an insecure woman, I would've taken her statement to heart. I would've let it eat at me until it created doubt in what I was building with Ace. Thankfully, insecure was something I never was or would ever be. What I had to offer was what I had to offer. If that wasn't more than enough for Ace, then he was not meant for me. "We're good but thank you for your concern."

Harmony ate her food in silence as Angel shook her head. "Mon, you really need to stop. How many times have I told you not to do that?"

"Do what? I was only trying to give her some womanly advice." Monica stated without an ounce of sincerity.

That was her second time bringing up her past with Ace, and I was sure the more time I spent around her it wouldn't be the last. Thankfully today was the last day that I did have to spend with her for Angel's sake.

"Woman to woman; your advice isn't needed," I replied before Angel could.

Harmony, Angel's cousin, began to snicker causing Monica to lower her head in embarrassment. Angel quickly changed the subject, so we were all able to enjoy the rest of our lunch. Well, at least three of us were able to. Monica sat in her seat sulking the rest of the time.

"ARE YOU NERVOUS?" I WHISPERED TO ANGEL. THE ALL white party was being held in the backyard of the house and had been going on for about an hour. All of Saint and Ace's childhood friends and family were in attendance. Cousins, aunts, uncles, and even the neighbors were at the party. There was one large tent where the food was being housed. The yard was covered with tables and chairs. Saint even had a wooden dance floor built. There were lights and white roses everywhere. St. Lucian music filled the air, and everyone was swaying to it. Off to the side, there was a large projector that he had set up.

The slideshow of Angel over the years that Saint had prepared was now playing. Angel had me add a few slides of the new baby's sonogram. The twins had shirts that read big sister and big brother with her due date on them. My phone was in hand while I waited on my cue to text the nanny and let her know when to bring them out. We thought it would be cute to have them flown out to be part of the surprise. Angel even went to the extent of making sure they napped all day so that they would be wide awake by the time the original slide show finished.

"Very nervous. I'm just ready to see the smile on his face." No sooner than Angel finished her statement the first slide of the sonogram showed. Saint's eyes narrowed as he looked at the slide. As soon as the second slide played, he turned to face Angel in confusion.

"I didn't add any slides of the twin's sonograms in there." He started speed walking towards where the projector was located. By this time, everybody was confused while Angel and I sat next to each other quietly giggling as I texted the nanny.

As soon as he made it to the projector, the twins came running full force out of the back door straight towards him. The second he noticed their shirts he looked at Angel for an explanation. SJ was wearing a white shirt with the words big brother on the front in blue. Heaven had an identical shirt with the words big sister in pink.

Angel now had the microphone in her hand, "Babe I love you so much. You have been everything to me over these past eight years." Her voice began to crack. "Saint you always outdo yourself for my birthday, but we're not just celebrating us tonight. We are celebrating a miracle, our Miracle."

With both SJ and Heaven in his arms, Saint took off towards Angel. He didn't try to wipe away his tears of joy. He didn't try to hide the fact that he was sobbing. His mission was getting to Angel. Once he made it to her, he handed the twins to me, "Are you for real?"

"I'm seventeen weeks babe. She'll be here in February of next year." "She?" Saint broke down even more.

"She is our Miracle."

Saint dropped to his knees and rested his head on

Angel's stomach. Everyone was talking, cheering, crying, or doing all three. The moment that the two was sharing was magical. It felt good to know that she trusted me enough to be part of it.

After their exchange, everyone crowded around them taking turns to congratulate the couple on the new addition to their family. It was amazing to witness the love that poured from everyone on to them. The party continued until three in the morning. Right after it ended, Ace and I returned to our room.

"That was beautiful."

"When do you feel like you'll be ready for that?" Ace asked. The party had long ended, and I had just gotten out of the shower. He was lying in bed wearing just a pair of black boxer briefs. My eyes traced the muscles of his arms that rested behind his head. His chest and beautifully sculpted abs served as the perfect distraction from answering his question.

"Di, did you not hear me?"

I did hear him. I was just unsure how to answer the question. When it came to marriage with Ace, I was ready for it yesterday. Ace was the man that I was going to marry. My heart had already given herself to him freely. Children, however, I wasn't so sure about. For as long as I could remember I told myself that children would have to come after I'd accomplished every goal that I set forth. Now, I was wondering if it was possible to have one before I had my own chain of restaurants. It had only been four months since I started working at Chez Saint, so my career had barely begun.

Making my way to the bed, I slid my body underneath his once I was under the

comforter. Ace hated covering, but I needed a comforter

no matter how high the temperature was. My body began to dissolve against his as I rested my head on his bare chest. Needing

clarification, I asked, "Ready for what exactly?" "For marriage and to start a family."

Before today we had spoken about marriage and children a few times. We touched the surface of it but never really went in depth. He and I both wanted the same things: love, marriage, and family. We never discussed a timeline, but we knew that was what we both wanted ultimately.

Ace and I practiced natural birth control. If done properly, it could be very effective. We monitored my menstrual cycle and did our best to refrain from sex during my ovulation period. We gave in a couple of times, but for the most part, we were strict. Neither one of us wanted a barrier in between us when we made love. I wasn't comfortable with the idea of artificial birth control due to the hormones and possible side effects.

"That's a hard question to answer. I want those things with you, but I can't really say when I will be ready to start a family." Starting a family wasn't something I foresaw in the near future. My career always came first, and I wasn't ready for anything or anyone else to take that place yet. With Ace, he allowed me to keep our relationship separate from that. Getting married and having children would change everything.

"You don't have to know right at this very moment Beauty. Those are things I want with you as well. We don't need to put a time on it. I just want to make sure we're on the same page and still want the same things. We're forever remember?" His full dark lips slowly curled into a smile.

"How could I forget? Forever." I fell asleep listening to the melodic rhythm of his heartbeat.

The next morning everything went by pretty fast, almost in a blur. Ace woke me up to breakfast in bed. He had finally cooked for me. Well, at least he claimed he had because I didn't witness him do it. Either way, the waffles were a golden brown just how I liked them. The omelet had all my favorite vegetables in it, and the bowl of tropical fruit provided me with the perfect sweetness. The freshly made passion fruit juice was made courtesy of his mom because he hadn't mastered juice making yet.

When I was done eating, he led me to the bathroom where he had a bath filled with yellow rose petals with red tips waiting for me. Ace requested that I allowed him to undress me and bathe me. I stood there in admiration as he took his time to undress me and help me into the bathtub.

"What's the meaning of the color?"

"Falling in love." That's all he said. No further explanation. An explanation that I needed to desperately hear. My eyes begged him to say more, but his lips refused. He bathed me as we let the silence consume us both. His strong hands roamed every inch of my body as if they were exploring it for the first time. They glided across my skin so gently and smoothly. The sensuality of his touch almost bringing me to climax led me to close my eyes.

"Don't fall asleep Di. It's time to get out and get dressed anyway. We're spending the day at Vigie Beach today."

My eyes quickly popped opened. "The beach?"

"Yeah crazy girl. Don't act like you haven't been to a beach before."

"I mean, I have, but it's been over two years." Since moving back from Michigan, I hadn't gotten the chance to go. The beach was absolutely my favorite place to be. There was something about the smell of the water and the sound of the waves that always brought a calmness to me.

"That's why we're going Beauty."

Ace helped me out of the tub and handed me a towel. When I made it to the bathroom, there was a yellow two-piece string bikini waiting for me on the bed.

"You know I brought plenty of bathing suits, right? You didn't have to buy one." Shrugging his shoulders, Ace replied, "Yellow looks good on your chocolate skin." To

him, his logic made sense, so I chose not to argue with it. Soon after getting dressed, Ace and I

headed to Vigie Beach. I wore the bikini he had purchased with a white cover-up. He wore

matching yellow swim trucks with a white shirt. Even though he thought it was corny to match each other, he knew I loved doing those kinds of things.

The beach was completely different from the beaches in Miami. Vigie Beach had a different type of atmosphere. We spent the entire day on the beach swimming, eating, and relaxing. It was the most perfect day. There wasn't stress or any pressure. It was almost as if he had forgotten that he pretty much told me he was in love with me. As badly as I wanted to bring it up, I didn't want to ruin the moment. Nor was I ready to admit that I had already fallen in love with him.

After a long and fun day at the beach, we returned to his parents' house. Our flight to return to Miami was early the next day. I wanted to make sure I got enough rest so that I wouldn't fall asleep during the flight back. The only thing I wanted to do was take a shower and cuddle next to Ace until I fell asleep. However, Ace had other plans.

He opened the bedroom door revealing a small red gift bag sitting in the middle of the bed. This man was so full of surprises. He had a mischievous grin on his face as he used his right hand to stroke his full beard.

"You are too much," I said while shaking my head. Ace did all these things for me, and all he ever wanted was my time, affection, and home-cooked meals. But whenever he did things like this, I felt like what I gave him wasn't enough

"Nothing I'll ever do for you will be too much Di. Just go get it."

There was a small box which I was sure was a Pandora charm to add to my bracelet as well as a greeting card. Over the past few months, he had given me so many cards, I had to get a second box just for him. Sure enough, it was a circular peach charm inside of the box.

Ace sauntered over to me and began removing the bracelet from my wrist. "Love. That's what the charm stands for Di. When I first told you I was falling for you, I had already fallen. When I see my future, you are the only person that I see by my side. I wanted you four months ago, I want you today, and I'll want you twenty years from now. I want you forever Beauty because I love you."

It took everything in me not to shed tears of happiness. Ace evoked so many emotions in me; it almost didn't make sense. I had never been an emotional person but leave it to Ace to make me turn to a cry baby. There was absolutely nothing sexier than a man that is sure of what he wants.

"Baby, you have no idea how much these gestures mean to me. You are a man of your word. Your actions never contradict what you tell me, and there is value in that. I love you too." His soft lips came crashing onto mine as he lifted me by my thighs giving me full access to wrap my legs around his waist.

"I love you Beauty."

"I love you too baby."

18

Ladi

PREGNANT. FIVE PREGNANCY TESTS ON MY BATHROOM floor confirmed it, but I still didn't want

to believe it. Three weeks after returning from St. Lucia, I was now sitting on the toilet seat in my bathroom staring at five plus signs. Five positive pregnancy tests. Three weeks. All which meant I was pregnant before I left for St. Lucia. The loud knock on the door startled me, causing me to jump from the toilet seat.

"Give me a second!"

"Are you ok? You've been in there for a long time." Chasity's voice came from the other side of the bathroom door.

"Yeah, I'll be out in a bit." Grabbing the tests, I stuffed them all in my purse that I had dropped on the floor. As soon as I opened the door, Chasity rushed past me.

"About time. What were you doing in the bathroom?"

"Using it," I replied over my shoulder as I walked to my room. Telling Chasity that I was pregnant was out of the question. Especially since I still didn't want to believe it. The only way I was going to believe it was after a doctor confirmed it with an ultrasound. The blood test I had gotten done last week wasn't even enough. The moment the blood test came back positive, my doctor scheduled the ultrasound. Yet here I was, still taking at home pregnancy tests. Almost as if it would miraculously disappear.

Chasity followed me to my room. "What's wrong with you?"

"Nothing Chas, just tired. I have to get ready for work, and then I have a doctor's appointment today to get a pap smear." Chasity and I had the same gynecologist, so I went ahead and told her where I was going. Plus, I wanted to save myself from her asking me a bunch of questions.

"I thought you were off."

"Was off. Chris has to come in late, so I'm covering for him." "Oh, I have an appointment today too."

She continued talking, but I was no longer listening. My mind was on getting through the four-hour shift at work, my doctor's appointment, and then how to tell Ace that I was pregnant once the ultrasound confirmed it.

Chas stood in the doorway talking while I got dressed for work. It was hard enough sneaking around my aunt, but thankfully she was at work since she started back part time last week. Adding Chas to the mix was another story. Chasity always had one hundred and one questions. She started spending more time with her sister, so she was around less. However,

every time she got back from hanging out with her all

she wanted to talk about was how Ace was going to break my heart.

Ace still hadn't given me any reason to believe that he would hurt me. Everything between us had only improved since St. Lucia. Our relationship was stable, and both of our careers were progressing. During our date last night, he showed me the building he had designed for my first restaurant as well as giving me a key to his new house that was now finished. He called it our home. Our home.

And here I was about to throw a baby at him. The bad part was that we were careful. Natural birth control was very effective which only meant I miscalculated when I ovulated. Either way, it felt like it was too early to have a baby and we were way too busy. I was sure we could make it work, but this was not a part of my plan.

Once I was fully dressed in a black high waisted pencil skirt, matching button-down blouse, and black flats, I pulled my hair into a high bun. I took my purse from my bed and I headed towards the front door. "I'll talk to you later Chas."

I rushed out of the house so that I could go and get the four hours at work out the way. The minute I made it to work, I knew that my short shift was going to be a tiring one. Two of my servers and one of the cooks called out. So I ended up being acting general manager, cook, and a server. By the time my shift was over the last thing I wanted to do was go to my OB, but I didn't have a choice.

As I parked my car at the OB office, I noticed Chas had sent me a text asking the time of my appointment. Remembering that she had an appointment today as well, I sent her a quick reply letting her know I just made it to the doctor's office. Nervousness consumed my entire body as I slowly made my way through the tall glass double doors. After signing in, I sat down waiting for my name to be called. It didn't take any longer than ten minutes for me to get called to the back.

"Ms. Thomas, how are you feeling today?" Dr. Tompkins voice was joyful, the complete opposite of what I was feeling on the inside. She was a tall, slim older woman with a short gray afro. Her flawless walnut complexion would have you second guessing her age.

"Truthfully?"

"Yes." Her reply made me chuckle. If it were Ace, he would've said he always wanted

the truth from me. I released a deep breath, "The ultrasound is the only thing that can make me believe that this is real. This isn't how I imagined things would go nor is it what I wanted. I'm anxious because I know once I see it, I won't want anything but it."

Speaking it out loud made me realize what my true fear was. It wasn't that I couldn't accomplish all of the goals that I had set forth. My fear was that I would be happy putting them on hold for my baby. My fear was the realization that I needed more than my career and degrees to truly fulfill me. This baby and Ace were my fulfillment.

"You've got this Ms. Thomas. Now lay back for me."

I laid back as she instructed. She squeezed a quarter-sized amount of the ultrasound gel on my lower abdomen and then used the probe to spread it. Soon after, an image approximately the size of a small grape appeared on the screen.

"There it is. It looks like you're measuring at nine weeks — very strong heartbeat. Everything looks good Ms. Thomas."

So many thoughts ran through my mind. When I heard the heartbeat, I knew it was meant to be. My belief was everything happened when it was supposed to. Ace asking me when I

would be ready for a family in St. Lucia was the preparation of putting me in the mindset for

what I was seeing right now, our baby. It happened faster than I thought it would, but it definitely happened when it was meant to happen.

Dr. Thompkins printed the sonogram for me once our appointment was over. The second I went to put them in my purse, my phone began to vibrate. Chasity's name appeared on the screen. I went to ignore her call but chose not to.

"Hey, Chas."

"Ladi, come outside right now! You need to see this!" Chas was yelling so loud I had to

pull the phone away from my ear.

"Stop yelling Chas. What's going on?"

"I'm in the lobby. Hurry up and come out here!" Hearing the urgency in her voice, I hurriedly left the room and went to the lobby,

The moment we saw each other, Chasity rushed to me grabbing my wrist as she dragged me towards the same double doors that I had walked through forty-five minutes ago. "What is wrong with you?"

"If I told you, you wouldn't believe me! You need to see and hear this for yourself."

Chasity looked like a crazy person with her gray sweats and a white tank top. Her wavy hair was down to her back and all over the place. She didn't look like she had a doctor's appointment today.

"Ace you are going to do right by me!" That high pitch squeaky voice was one I would never forget. Sasha.

"You have really lost it, Sasha."

"I'm pregnant, and you owe it to me and our baby to be there." I watched as Ace's mouth fell open and looked down at Sasha's small round belly. She couldn't have been any more than five months. That meant he lied about the last time they were together if she was claiming him as the father of her child. He didn't deny it.

It felt like a thousand daggers were thrown at my body tearing me into a million pieces. A coldness swept over me which gave the strength I needed to speak, but the only word that I could form was, "Wow."

Ace's head whipped around fast causing his dreads to barely miss hitting Sasha. This masterpiece of a man that my heart had given herself to so freely was now the reason for her death. "Di."

He took a step towards me as I took one away. There were no words to speak. There were no tears to cry. This was not the time because emotions were running high. Sasha had a satisfied

smirk as if she had won some grand prize. Turning around, I took off running towards my car. Ace had a delayed response and didn't follow me immediately. Right as he made it to my car, I already had the car in drive. Ignoring him yelling my name and banging my window, I drove away to clear my head.

That's when it hit me harder than a ton of bricks, I was carrying his child as well.

❦ 19 ❦

Ace

"WHAT THE FUCK!" I YELLED AT THE TOP OF MY LUNGS. Why did this keep happening to me? I needed to release the rage that began to sneak up. This was the most excruciating pain I had ever felt in my life. My heart literally felt like it was being ripped out of my chest. My vision went black as I clutched my chest. My breathing became heavy and sporadic as my mind went wild wondering how to fix this. Sasha's and Chasity's laughter momentarily broke me out of my daze.

"You!" I went charging towards Sasha with my finger pointing at her. "You set me up!" "You deserve it! Did you think I was going to let you get away with being happy with her?" Sasha asked, and Chasity's laughter grew louder.

"And you!" I quickly turned towards Chasity "You helped her set me up. You helped her break Ladi's heart.

189

Why?" I wanted to hurt both of them, but the man that I was wouldn't let me.

"I'm her sister. What do you think?" Sasha answered which only made Chasity laugh harder. That's when it dawned on me, Chasity was Sasha's younger sister. That's why she looked familiar. I had seen her picture at Sasha's mom's house the one time that I went there.

"I don't care about you being my sister. Blood means nothing to me. Why does Ladi get to be happy while I'm broken? I deserve happiness not her and especially not Sasha. Sasha is a hoe and Ladi is naïve! We are the ones that should be together because I deserve a good man!"

Sasha's face turned red as she balled up her hands. Neither one of us could believe the trash that was spewing out of Chasity's mouth. Envy could make the prettiest person ugly.

"Both of you are sick! I swear if I lose Ladi for good, both of you are going to pay. Sasha go find your baby's father because you know you and I haven't slept together in almost a year. Chasity, you stay away from Ladi." As soon as I turned my back, Chasity went flying to the ground. I stood there briefly as the two fought one another. Security came running outside to separate the two as I made my way to my car.

Once inside, I pulled out my phone to call Ladi. In the back of mind, I knew she wouldn't answer, but I called anyway. It rung four times and just when I was about hang up to call again, she answered. She didn't speak, but she answered.

"Di let me explain, please. Can I see you?"

"No. I don't want to hear any explanations right now. What I need is time. When I'm ready to talk, then we will talk."

"Please Di, I'm begging you Beauty."

"Bye Ace." Just like that, she hung up. When I tried calling her again, it went straight to voicemail. Throwing my phone on the passenger seat, I started up my car to drive to her house. There was no way I could wait for her to want to talk to me. It was impossible for me to get through this day and not have access to her. Ladi never fought me, but she was now restricting herself from me. I couldn't blame her, but I'd be damn if it didn't hurt like hell.

Sasha set me up, and I let her. She called me from a different phone number, crying and apologizing. She had me convinced that she had finally taken ownership for our failed relationship. I went against my better judgment when she asked that I meet up with her, so she could do it in person. When Sasha sent me the address to a public place and not her house, I thought she was for real. Clearly, I was wrong. Our conversation was normal when we first

started talking. I had even congratulated her on her pregnancy. It was like a switch went off in her head when she knew Ladi was there. She flipped the switch and tried to pin a baby on me that we both knew wasn't mine.

Chastity obviously knew Ladi was going to be at the doctor's office and she helped Sasha set the whole thing up. Ladi did tell me she had a doctor's appointment but never in a million years did I think that it was the doctor's office Sasha wanted me to meet her at. Because it was last minute when I agreed to meet with Sasha, I had planned on telling Ladi about it after it happened.

My phone started to vibrate, and I almost wrecked my car grabbing it to answer hoping that it was Ladi. Disappointment overwhelmed me when Saint's name appeared on the screen.

"What's up, this isn't a good time," I answered

"Have you been on Facebook?"

"No, why?"

"Sasha and Chasity are getting arrested right now. It's on Facebook."

It had only been fifteen minutes since I left. "You sure?" I asked.

"There was a full out brawl out there. Hold on." The video was playing in the background, but I couldn't make out what they were saying. "Yeah, it's definitely them. Another pregnant girl got arrested too. She and Sasha are pregnant by the same guy." He started laughing and had I been in a better mood, I would've been laughing with him.

Before he could question my mood, I asked, "You at home or at work?" "Work, why?"

"I need a drink. Heading your way now." And hung up.

The parking lot of Chez Saint wasn't too crowded when I arrived since it was four in the afternoon on a Tuesday. Defeat was written all over my face. Ladi's phone was still going to voicemail, but that didn't deter me from calling and sending multiple text messages. All I needed her to do was answer her phone.

Stopping by the bar first, I ordered a coke and rum before heading to Saint's office. "Why do you look like that?" he asked as soon as I sat down across from him. "Sasha and Chasity set me up."

"When did you start back talking to Sasha?" Sighing heavily, I ran my hand down my face. Starting from the call I got from Sasha, Saint listened tentatively as I explained how everything played out.

He shook his head, "There's no possibility that the baby is yours?"

"No man, I would never cheat on Di. You know that.

Now Ladi is somewhere thinking I cheated on her." I finished up my drink while continuing to sulk in my chair.

"Just give her space. You know Ladi, and you didn't do anything wrong. Sasha and Chasity are both crazy. I still can't believe they're sisters. How did Ladi not know that."

"They aren't close. The reason I figured it out was because Sasha said it and then I remembered seeing a picture at their mom's house. They slightly favor but not really."

"That's just wild. Just give her space and you better not bring that drama to Chez Saint or

I'm beating your ass." He started laughing, and I couldn't help but join him.

"Appreciate you man."

"Anytime, now go home and wait for Ladi to call you. She will."

"Bet." I stood up to leave although I didn't have any intentions of going home. My only destination was Ladi's house. If I had to spend every day out there until she decided to speak to me, that was exactly what I planned to do.

❧ 20 ❧

L adi

"LADI, WHAT'S WRONG WITH YOU?" MY AUNT HAD JUST gotten back from work and kept asking me a million questions. I had been at home for two hours and managed to make dinner, so she wouldn't have to.

"Nothing is wrong Auntie Marie. Do you want me to fix your plate?" Auntie Marie was feeling a lot better. Whenever she went back for a scan after the surgery, everything came back normal. She was doing great, working less, and I was grateful.

"When you're ready to talk, I'm here cherie. I'll eat later after my nap."

I did need to talk but the person I needed to talk to, was the one person I didn't want to talk to. Numbness was the only thing I felt when trying to come to terms with the fact that Ace had cheated on me and had another baby on the way. Another baby by another woman. That brought me back to the conversation that Chasity and I had before she moved back to Miami. No one should have to experience this level of hurt.

Chasity hadn't called me since the whole incident took place. When I got home all of her things were gone. She had mentioned moving out weeks ago but never brought it back up. When I tried calling her phone, it went straight to voicemail. My phone was turned off because I knew Ace would try calling me and I couldn't talk to him right now. I desperately wanted to tell him I was pregnant but, how could I? It would have to wait until I was ready.

There was a knock on the door, but when I went to open it, there was only an I'm sorry greeting card with a single yellow rose laying on the mat. Ace. That single gesture shouldn't have made my heart melt, but it did. It was sweet, but it wasn't enough to forgive his betrayal. The note read:

BEAUTY, I LOVE YOU. EVERYTHING ISN'T AS IT SEEMS. *Believe me when I tell you I would never cheat on you or do anything to deliberately hurt you. Your heart was the greatest gift that you could have given me. I cherish it just as I cherish you. You aren't talking to me, so I have to explain myself through written words. I never cheated on you. Sasha is not having my child. You are the*

only woman that will ever be able to say that. I need you. I'm begging you Di. Please, come to the car and talk to me, mama.

LOOKING UP, I NOTICED ACE SITTING ON THE HOOD OF

his car watching me read the card from across the street. The sadness in his eyes transcended to his tall stature. The dark chocolate man that held so much power in his stance resembled a lost child. His broad muscular shoulders were hunched over. His long beautiful dreads hung loosely over his head making no effort to hide his red eyes. He looked exactly how I felt. Broken.

As I walked over to him, he raised his arms in an attempt to pull me into his embrace. I stopped before I was in his reach. The last thing I needed was to become weak to his touch right now. The only thing I needed was answers, yet I found myself asking what the yellow rose signified.

"Friendship and new beginnings. That's what I want for us."

"She's pregnant. I saw it, and you didn't deny it being yours." My arms were folded across my chest. I had changed from my work clothes to a blue pair of his shorts and a black tank top.

Ace ran his hand down his face. "She is, but it's not mine. We haven't had sex in almost a year, Di. You have to believe me."

"Why would you meet with her and not tell me? Did you not think that would make it look like you're hiding something?"

"It does. Meeting up with her was stupid, but she called apologizing and asked for closure. When she gave me the address to a public place, I thought she was being genuine. It was last minute, but I was going to tell you about it afterward Di."

He went on to explain how Chasity was involved in setting him up. My best friend tried to ruin my happiness because she was in pain. He then pulled out his phone to show the viral video of them getting arrested on Facebook. I felt stupid and mortified. Ace didn't break my trust, Chasity did. It all made sense why she was stuck on Ace not being good for me. Sasha was her older sister, and she never made an effort to share that with me.

"Can we please have a new beginning Beauty. No more Sasha, rumors from your job, no more Monica, no more Chasity. Just you and I?"

Ace was pleading with his words and his eyes. His words embedding seeds of hope that I wanted to watch grow for the rest of my life. "No."

His head fell to his chest, and I used my hand to raise his head up. Using my other hand, I pulled the sonogram out of the pocket of the basketball shorts. "We can have a new beginning with the three of us, June of next year."

EPILOGUE

E pilogue: One year later

ACE

"YOU CAN PUT HIM DOWN, BABY." LADI AND I WERE hosting a dinner at our home to celebrate the life of our son who was almost two months old. He looked identical to her. I should've known that she had strong genes based on how much she and Auntie Marie resembled one another. The only things he inherited from me were my dark eyes and complexion.

"I know I can, but I don't want to." I kissed her on the forehead before leaving the bedroom to finish getting ready.

A lot had changed for us in a year. She and I moved into the house that I had designed when she was seven months pregnant. We paid off her aunt's house so that she would no longer have a mortgage. Auntie Marie was still working part-time at the hospital. Ladi finally accepted that she couldn't stop that. The design that I created for Ladi's restaurant was now a reality. She wanted to wait until AJ, Ace Jr., was six months before getting into it. Saint was upset to see her go after her maternity leave, but she did a great job of training Ashley to take her position.

Many holidays and birthdays had passed, giving us many memories. Every day with her was better than the last. The moment Di pulled the sonogram out of her pocket, my love for her grew more than I knew was possible. She was everything to me, and I lived every day proving that to her. She had twenty-three of the twenty-four charms of the Essence Collection from Pandora. Tonight, I was going to give her the last one to complete the collection.

Everyone was in the dining room waiting for us. My parents had flown into town for the celebration. Auntie Marie was seated next to my mom. Saint was there with Angel and the twins. Miracle had made her debut months before AJ. She was snuggled tightly in my mom's arms. Ladi didn't want a formal dinner. We disagreed about it for weeks until she finally gave in and agreed to a formal dinner like I wanted.

"Let me have him." my mom said once I sat at the head of the table.

"Ma, you have Miracle." Everyone started laughing because she was trying to reach for him while holding Miracle in one arm.

"Give me Miracle Ma, you can get AJ." Saint offered.

"No, I want them both. That is how I would hold the twins. Now give me AJ." Shaking my head, I strolled over to her, placing AJ in her free arm.

Ladi finally arrived at the dining room fifteen minutes

later wearing a yellow, skintight, knee-length, off-the-shoulder lace dress. She knew exactly how much I loved her wearing yellow. It made her skin glow. The dressed caressed each curve on her body perfectly.

Before she could sit down, I walked up to her. "I want to give you something before you sit down Beauty." I removed a small box out of my pocket and opened it showcasing the smooth red circular charm. "This represents energy. The energy that you bring into my life is what keeps me going daily. I once thought that the greatest gift you could've given me was your heart. You proved me wrong when you gave birth to our son."

She had two Pandora bracelets on her wrist. The one that I purchased originally couldn't take any more charms, so I had purchased a second one. She slipped the bracelet from her arm and handed it to me. Taking it from her, I added the energy charm and positioned it back on her wrist.

"Baby, if I know one thing, it's that men like you are rare. I'm grateful for you. When I doubt anything, you give me certainty. For that and many other reasons, I love you."

That was Ladi's greatest gift, the ability to touch my soul with her words. Pulling her into a tight hug, I laid a soft kiss on her forehead. As she removed herself from my grasp, I said, "Today I want to prove me wrong for a third time."

Ladi began to look around the room with a look of confusion that matched everyone else's. No one knew what my plans were. My love and life with Ladi were the most sacred things to me. There were certain parts I didn't want to share, I wanted them reserved for just the two of us. This was one of those moments, but I had been waiting over a year to do it. I didn't want to wait a second longer.

"I want you to prove me wrong by giving me the greatest gift next to our son. Give me your hand in marriage." I got down on one knee and pulled out the three-carat, cushion-cut, fancy yellow and white diamond frame engagement ring that I had bought the day she said yes to making us official. We both knew she was going to be my wife, but we needed time to teach each other more about this love that we had been fostering.

"Beauty will you..."

"Yes! Yes, I will marry you." Laughter took over the room because I couldn't even get the question out.

Shaking my head with a smile that matched hers, I continued, "Today?" "What?"

"Say you'll marry me today." I took her hand and led her to the back. There were enough white chairs for our family. Red and yellow roses adorned the ground and arch. It was intimate and elegant. There were wooden structures with a timeline of our relationship. The rustic ambiance was something that I didn't particularly care for, but Ladi was in love with it. Everything that Ladi had described that she wanted whenever I asked what her dream wedding was six months, I made sure was recreated in our backyard.

"Red and yellow roses together represent happiness and excitement. That is what our marriage will be filled with."

She drew me down to her plump lips and started to kiss me passionately. Only removing her lips to say, "I'll marry you today because we're forever."

"Forever Beauty."

The End

9 781698 854762